A MIGHTY AFTERNOON

A MIGHTY AFTERNOON

CHARLES K. MILLS

DOUBLEDAY & COMPANY, INC.
GARDEN CITY, NEW YORK
1980

First Edition

ISBN: 0-385-17194-3
Library of Congress Catalog Card Number 80-1037
Copyright © 1980 by Charles K. Mills
All Rights Reserved
Printed in the United States of America

Departed to the judgment
A MIGHTY AFTERNOON
Great clouds like ushers leaning
Creation looking on . . .
  —Emily Dickinson (1830–86)

A MIGHTY AFTERNOON

Thursday, June 22, 1876

It was the first day of summer, but it might have been the first day of spring for all the cool, blustery weather. A very heavy, cold north wind pushed at the backs of the mounted soldiers. Though almost noon, it was grim and dark as the horses clip-clopped up the stony slope of the barren tableland away from the Yellowstone River toward the sandy, sagebrush-dotted foothills flanking the narrow, winding Rosebud River.

The cavalry column came on four abreast by companies. Behind them, the twisting Yellowstone separated them from the infantry and cavalry of Colonel John Gibbon's Montana Column. Gibbon's men had been ferried north by the stern-wheeler steamboat *Far West*, which was once again moored on the south bank, waiting for the last of the northern detachment.

The men of that detachment were mounted, watching the twelve companies of the U.S. 7th Cavalry march past. Three of them were seated more or less comfortably on their horses ahead of the others, close enough for the general to call out personal greetings to the commanders of the companies of the 7th Cavalry. The general was Alfred Howe Terry, a middle-aged former lawyer who had served with distinction in the Civil War and remained in the postwar frontier Army to command the Department of Dakota, a command that covered three present-day states: North and South Dakota and Montana.

General Terry was a tall, erect man with a noticeably thickened waistline and hair that was powdered gray. He had the face of a basset hound, an impression belied by the brightness of his eyes. His hair was short; his beard, small but thick. Even in the wilderness there was something of the dandy about him.

There was nothing dandified about the man mounted to his immediate right. Colonel John H. Gibbon had been a division commander during the Civil War and was reduced in the postwar Army to the command of a single infantry regiment. He was a lean, sharp-nosed man in his early forties with an apparently complete disregard for his own appearance. A sack tunic coat, unbuttoned, covered ill-fitting trousers, effectively concealing a crippled hip that caused him to limp painfully. He nodded as the carelessly garbed Indian scouts in the van of the 7th Cavalry circled with their ponies and generally performed what appeared to be acrobatics with solemn faces, accompanied by a keening, mournful chant.

On Terry's left sat a leathery, hunched man with a round, seamy face almost too small for his body. He looked in pain and probably was to some extent, due to arthritis, but it wasn't as severe as his weather-beaten features made it seem. He was Major James S. Brisbin of the 2nd Cavalry and only the night before he had been denied a place in the column parading before him. He had protested, but only as a matter of form, and viewed the parade with his customary pinched, painful expression. He was known as "Grasshopper Jim" throughout the Army.

All the trumpeters of the 7th Cavalry—two to a company and mounted on gray horses—led by Chief Trumpeter Voss, a blond-haired, blue-eyed German, swung 270 degrees to their left, ending up facing the reviewing party they had just marched past. They played "Garryowen" in the brassy, strident tones that bugles, or trumpets, unaccompanied always give forth. Still, it was stirring in a crude way.

The Indian scouts were accompanied by five white men in rough frontiersman clothing—all distinctly different, yet oddly alike. One was a mere boy; one, a middle-aged man with wind-burned cheeks and sharp black eyes. The rest were in their late twenties or early thirties, lean, bronzed, and hard-looking. There was a Negro with the scouts also: a black man with kinky white hair and a solemn expression. At least three of the Indians were obviously half-breeds and the remainder were dressed in cast-off government issue and civilian clothes so as to render any tribal affiliation of the scouts unrecognizable. There were, in fact, a few Sioux among them—without exception older men who were not expected to fight by the dictates of their own culture, but apparently they sought action for its own sake—even to the extreme of fighting their own people. There were a half dozen Crows with the scouts. They had been loaned to the 7th Cavalry by Colonel Gibbon because they knew the country well. They were taller than the rest of the Indians, with long handsome profiles and long black hair tossed back in a pompadour. Four were youngsters with little experience; the other two were middle-aged men. They were all dressed in a curious mixture of cast-off government issue and fancy beaded buckskin. They rode government horses.

The rest of the Indians were Arikarees, called Rees. They were solemn, bowlegged, dark-skinned little men mounted on Indian ponies. Most were young with little or no experience, but sprinkled among them were older, more experienced warriors. They trotted past the three-officer reviewing party, seemingly oblivious to the effect they produced, singing in a strange minor key that was oddly in harmony with the brassy notes of "Garryowen."

The sharp-featured officer who led the scouts dropped his salute and relaxed his unnaturally squared shoulders perceptibly. Second Lieutenant Charles Albert Varnum was twenty-seven years old and a graduate of West Point (class of '72). This was his third Indian campaign and already he had a reputation for ferocity in combat. Tall and slender like a fence post, he had a wide forehead, almost beady dark eyes, a small pointed chin, and a thin, pointed nose. His mouth was small and seemed perpetually pursed. The ragged Indians he commanded nicknamed him "Peaked Face," which was appropriate. He had grown a small brush mustache that accentuated his sharp dark eyes and he had the beginnings of a beard, which looked like what it was: neglect of the razor for a month. Varnum wore a buckskin shirt and pants and a large gray wool felt civilian hat, pulled down low over his eyes.

Next in column was a small party—three sergeants, two of whom were bearing flags on nine-foot lances—led by two officers. The officers swung out and approached the three-man reviewing party, saluting.

"Very fine appearance, your people," said General Terry. "Very fine mounts, too, General Custer. Very fine animals."

Lieutenant Colonel (Brevet Major General) George Armstrong Custer was thirty-six and a half years old. His rise had been meteoric during the Civil War: a general at twenty-three, a cavalry division commander at twenty-five. He had survived countless skirmishes and battles, having eleven horses shot out from under him, though he had nothing more than a childhood scar on the forehead to show for it all. The son of a blacksmith, Custer had entered the Military Academy at West Point and graduated at the bottom of his class in June of 1861—just in time for the beginning of the Civil War. The "Boy General" was now a middle-aged man. He had reddish-blond hair and, as he swept off his low-crowned white wool hat, it was obvious that he was going to be bald in the not too distant future. He didn't take the sun too well, either—for what parts of his face and neck were not freckled were badly burned by a combination of sun and wind that gave him a boiled-lobster look. His nose was big and fleshy, his cheekbones high and prominent. A drooping walrus mustache, lighter in shade than his hair, almost completely obscured his thin pursed lips and a short, but bushy, reddish beard covered a receding chin. He was not a handsome man, and not particularly well dressed in his buckskin suit, but there was something arresting, commanding even, about his appearance. His eyes were blue and flashing, but this was only part of it. He was lean and athletically built and rode heels-down, toes-in like a man born to the saddle. The flowing golden tresses that had been his "Long Hair" trademark were nowhere in evidence. Varnum, the pinch-faced scout commander, had run horse clippers over them a month before and Custer's stuck-out ears were still quite visible.

When Custer spoke, his voice was high-pitched, almost girlish, and his words ran over each other separated only occasionally by a noticeable stammer.

"Thank you, General," he said. "Pity we had to dismount the band. The trumpeters look sharp enough, but they are no substitute for the real thing."

Terry nodded absently. "Yes, a band would be nice. But where you're going, they aren't essential and trumpeters are."

Custer flushed and replaced his wide-brimmed hat with a flourish. The officer beside him was dressed identically in buckskins, but there the similarity ended. While Custer looked like a buffalo hunter with too much sun, First Lieutenant William Winer Cooke looked like a cavalry regiment commander. He was, in fact, the adjutant: a tall, stately man with short hair and exceptionally long Dundreary side whiskers. Cooke was a Canadian, a Civil War veteran, and had been the adjutant for almost five years (including a brief stint in that capacity in Kansas). His foreign birth and guardsmanlike appearance had earned him the nickname "The Queen's Own" and he wheeled his large white horse expertly alongside his commander as they turned to watch the remainder of the regiment march past. Cooke sat as immobile as a Horse Guard at Whitehall, while Custer looked almost theatrically at the sergeant major and two banner-bearing sergeants who followed the scouts and preceded the column of fours that made up the twelve companies of the 7th Cavalry.

The sun was directly overhead, but obscured by the dense gray clouds from the north, as the companies walked past the impromptu reviewing party. The horses were large—fourteen to sixteen hands high and weighing from eight hundred to a thousand pounds. Grain-fed and sturdy, they represented a year's pay for the average soldier and many were obviously thoroughbred. They were branded US on the left shoulder and 7C on the left rump. Some had company designations burned into their hide above the regimental stamp. The trumpeters opposite the reviewing party all had gray mounts—mostly borrowed from the dismounted band— and the companies had originally been mounted on horses of the same color. Even now, the substitutes were few and far between and then mostly ridden by officers or recruits. The veteran enlisted men rode horses that had been assigned to them because of their color.

Company B was the first in column. They rode buckskin or bay horses for the most part. The breast straps and stirrup hoods had been removed and the small McClellan saddles were cinched tight to prevent them from sliding backward as the troops negotiated the incline. The saddles rested almost precariously on six-folded Army horse blankets—blue with yellow trim—and the accouterments were piled and strapped on in almost impossible bulk. The soldiers rode pigeon-toed, reins in left hand, straight-backed atop them.

The troops were a motley-looking group—more like a band of plainsmen riding in formation than an Army unit trained to respond by the numbers. They were dusty and whiskered and looked as if they had slept in their uniforms. It appeared at first glance that no two were dressed alike, but closer inspection revealed a kind of uniformity that government issue dictated. They wore dark blue blouses of at least four different kinds: from the pre-Civil War shell jacket with its choke collar and twelve brass buttons to the modern five-button blouse of 1874. The blouses were tucked into light blue kersey wool trousers, some reinforced with white canvas. Only the officers could afford civilian shirts or buckskin jackets—many of them handmade by loving wives. The individuality of the enlisted men was best manifested in their headgear. Most of them wore the almost shapeless regulation black hat, folded and creased a variety of ways according to individual taste. Some wore white wool hats with lower crowns and wider brims. Some wore cheap straw hats for protection from the sun (and little else), while others wore the misshapen kepi, or forage cap, issued to recruits.

Almost without exception, they wore wide leather slings with brass buckles at the left shoulder and steel rings on the right hip. Attached to the rings were Springfield single-shot .45-caliber carbines. They were the 1873 model, the "trap door," forty-one and some inches long, weighing six and a half pounds, and having an effective range of about three hundred yards. Each soldier carried a hundred rounds of ammunition—fifty on his person. They were secured either in the leather, half-moon-shaped Dyer cartridge cases or in a variety of "prairie belts"—loops of leather or canvas on wide belts of matching material. On their right hips—in a holster apparently designed for left-handed men—they carried Colt .45-caliber six-shot revolvers. There were no sabers in evidence.

Most wore yellow leather gauntlets. Some had reinforced their light blue woolen trousers with patches of white canvas. K Company, in the middle of the column, wore modified white canvas trousers made from stable overalls. Other individuals throughout the regiment followed the lead of the "dude troop," wearing handmade trousers that fit better and wore better than the government issue. Even up close, they looked better.

They rode in a column of fours preceded by one or two officers and a guidon bearer. The guidon was a simple swallowtail version of the American flag and, thus, all twelve were identical. They moved past the reviewing party quickly—some companies larger than others, but none approaching the authorized strength of sixty-four men for a cavalry company (as cavalry troops were officially called at that time).

The "Fighting Seventh" rolled on. The regiment had been in existence less than ten years and had spent only seven of those on the frontier policing Indians. Never before had all twelve companies been deployed together in a single column. Most of the service seen before had been that of small units pursuing hostiles with little or no contact made. In the seven years of frontier duty, the regiment had been in only thirty-two engagements. They had lost fewer than forty men during that period—more than half at a single battle: the Battle of the Washita. They had inflicted nearly two hundred casualties on the enemy Indians during that same period of time—again, more than half at the Washita. Discounting the Washita figures, the regiment in seven years had lost fewer than twenty men to Indians, while killing or wounding some one hundred Indians. It wasn't a particularly glorious record compared to the statistics of the older pre-Civil War units, but for the peacetime Army, it was as impressive a record as that of most other units.

The company commanders returned the greetings and good wishes of General Terry in distinctive ways that were oddly much alike. The company commanders were, without exception, combat veterans. Many of them had risen to such exalted ranks as colonel during the Civil War. After the war, they reverted to lowly lieutenants and, in rare instances, captains.

B Company on bay horses was commanded by Captain Thomas Mower McDougall. Captain Mac, as he was called, was the son of a general. He had left home at eighteen to join the Union Army and risen from the ranks to captain. After the war, he had to start all over again—this time, however, he began as a second lieutenant. McDougall was only thirty-one, but already losing a battle with his own waistline. Round-faced, thin-nosed, and with muttonchops of moderate length that were beginning to gray, he looked like a fat man who had drastically reduced. In fact, he was headed the other way: the proverbial thin man in a fat man's body. He had level blue eyes.

C Company was mounted on light sorrels and commanded by General Custer's younger brother, Captain Thomas Ward Custer.

There was a slight family resemblance, to be sure, but Tom Custer was inches taller than his more famous brother and had a truly hard-bitten look about him. Tom was thirty, a bachelor and "ranker" who had been commissioned from the ranks during the Civil War. He had been breveted to the rank of lieutenant colonel for bravery in action and had won the coveted Medal of Honor twice. A bullet wound marred his right cheek—earning him the nickname "Scar Face" among the Indian scouts. He had a flat, triangular face with narrow-set blue eyes and a sharp nose. He dressed in buckskin like his older brother and habitually wore his white hat low over his eyes.

E Company was mounted on gray horses, earning itself the nickname "Gray Horse Troop." General Terry had an especially warm greeting for its commander, First Lieutenant Algernon Emory Smith, for the simple reason that A. E. "Fresh" Smith had been Terry's aide during the Civil War. He was a New Yorker, thirty-three and a half, who had come up through the ranks during the war. A. E. Smith was a stocky man with a crippled shoulder. He had been badly wounded in the left shoulder during the war and still was unable to lift his left arm above it—making even such a simple task as putting on a jacket impossible without help. "Smithy," as he was also known, had sandy eyebrows, a wide, straight nose, and a heavy mustache. He had just recently been given command of the Gray Horse Troop.

F Company followed, mounted on bays. F Company was called the "Band Box Troop" for their exceptional appearance on the drill field. It was also the company with the highest percentage of German immigrants in its ranks. Captain George Walter Yates, a thickset blond with broad face and long prominent nose, commanded. Yates was thirty-three, a Civil War vet who had come up through the ranks. He was a Michigander—from Libbie Custer's hometown, Monroe—and had by chance served on Custer's staff throughout the war. He was part of the Custer "family." He even looked like Custer in a well-fed sort of way. He had the same coloring, walrus mustache, and even buckskin suit.

"Wild I" Company was mounted on bays also. An Irish soldier of fortune named Myles Walter Keough commanded. Captain Keough had been in the Italian (Papal) Army and also the Union Army. A tall, slender, curly-haired thirty-four-year-old with dark snapping eyes, a Vandyke beard, and a clipped mustache, he wore a buckskin shirt with blue trousers. His black hat matched his hair and small beard.

L Company was mounted on bays and commanded by General Custer's brother-in-law, First Lieutenant James Calhoun. "Jimmy" Calhoun was thirty, a hefty, broad-shouldered blond with an unusually square jaw and steely blue eyes. He had served in the Regular Army during the war as an enlisted man and had been promoted to officer from the ranks two years after it ended— a sign of remarkable ability in the rank-heavy postwar Army. Calhoun was considered the Adonis of the regiment, but four years of happily married life was beginning to show around his waist and neck. He wore a buckskin shirt and blue trousers and affected the low-over-the-eyes set for his white hat made popular by his other brother-in-law, Tom Custer.

A Company was next, mounted on black horses—earning for themselves the appellation "Black Horse Troop." They were also known as the "Forty Thieves," though there were, in fact, almost sixty of them, with the Irish, Germans, and other immigrants evenly divided. Captain Myles Moylan commanded. Moylan, a craggy-featured, beetle-browed man of thirty-seven and a half, was married to Jimmy Calhoun's sister Charlotte. His most distinctive feature was his long handlebar mustache that set off his arrestingly level blue eyes remarkably. Mylie Moylan had a checkered Army career that had included dismissal from the Civil War after being commissioned from the ranks. He had promptly re-enlisted under an assumed name and was promoted from the ranks once again. The war's end made him an enlisted man and he had joined the newly formed 7th Cavalry as a private. He was made regimental sergeant major within a month and was commissioned from the ranks yet again within three months.

D Company, on bay horses, was commanded by a Civil War lieutenant colonel made captain by the postwar austerity: Thomas Bell Weir. Captain Weir was thirty-eight, up from the ranks and a homely man who had served with Custer almost throughout his Army career. He was broad-shouldered, round-faced, and squint-eyed with stuck-out ears and a light, scraggly mustache. His nose was too big for his face and crooked as well. He was not in good health and hadn't been for some time, as his wearing a long gray overcoat showed.

G Company, on sorrels, had two distinctions: it was the only company with more immigrants than native Americans in its ranks and it was commanded by a part Indian. First Lieutenant Donald McIntosh was thirty-seven and a half—a Canadian-born ranker who had been given a commission from the ranks twice: once during the Civil War and once again immediately afterward. "Tosh" McIntosh was clean-shaven, broad-shouldered, and had high cheekbones and close-set brown eyes. He wore a kepi with the 7th Cavalry brass.

H Company had the fewest number of immigrants in its ranks and was mounted on blood bay horses. Captain Frederick William Benteen commanded. Forty-two-year-old Fred Benteen had been a full colonel and a cavalry brigade commander during the Civil War. A Southerner, he chose the Union side and had been commissioned directly from civilian life. He had refused to serve as major in a Negro cavalry regiment immediately after the war and had accepted a captaincy in the 7th Cavalry instead. Since the recent retirement of old Captain Thompson, clean-shaven, white-haired Fred Benteen had been the senior captain of the regiment. He was a combative-looking man with broad shoulders atop a short, stocky body and had the slightly bowed legs of a veteran horse soldier. His pugnacious jaw and large, piercing blue eyes were belied by an almost perpetual grin. The Indians had no name for him, but the troops referred to him as a "shaven Santa Claus." He wore a regulation blue tunic and battered black hat with studied nonchalance.

K Company, the smallest with fewer than forty-five men, was mounted on sorrels. They were the "dude troop" whose sartorial splendor featured the envied white canvas trousers made from stable clothes. It was the only company commanded by a West Pointer—First Lieutenant Edward Settle Godfrey. "Goddy" was thirty-three, a '67 graduate of the Military Academy and a veteran of nine years' frontier service. He was lean and spare with a very large nose and close-set dark eyes. A drooping mustache added to his aquiline features, which were spoiled only by a long, but sparse, beard.

The last company, M Company, rode mixed horses. Captain

Thomas Henry French commanded. "Tucker" French was a small, flat-faced man dressed in buckskin. His medium-sized, drooping mustache complemented his bushy dark eyebrows and he rode a large gray horse with the skill of a man apparently born in the saddle. In fact, though, French had been an infantryman during the Civil War and had been commissioned from the ranks while in the Regular Army. His obsidian eyes gave nothing away.

One officer and his orderly rode at the tail of the column—Major Marcus Albert Reno, West Point class of '57. The second-in-command normally "led the pelican"—that is, rode at the rear of the troops when he had no command of his own. Until the day before, Mark Reno had commanded six of the twelve companies on a scout, but, at odds with Custer, was now relegated to the rear. He was a tall, well-built man of forty-one with dark hair and a high protruding forehead. Though older than Custer by five years, he looked younger with his face clean-shaven except for a small mustache above thin lips. He wore the regulation blue sack-coat tunic over lighter blue coarse wool trousers tucked into short boots and a nearly shapeless straw hat that was tilted back to reveal the high dark forehead that had earned him the nickname "Man with a Dark Face" among the Indian scouts.

One hundred and sixty mules carrying clothes, food, and blankets in poorly loaded packsaddles and ammunition in leather aparejos straggled badly behind the blue column. A few unsaddled horses were mingled among them under the watchful eyes of a dozen civilian packers. After the magnificent display of the horse column, the packtrain was something of a disappointment. The reviewing party watched disdainfully, if a little resignedly, as two civilians cut out a mule whose pack had slipped. They retied the load over the mule's braying protest and, the ordeal over, released the mule to trot toward the bell mare ahead and easily regain its position in the column.

Major Reno rode over and exchanged a few stiff words with Custer—his eyes on the three-man reviewing party.

Custer turned to Cooke, the splendidly whiskered adjutant.

"My compliments to Captain French," he said in his high-pitched, rapid voice. "I want Lieutenant Mathey to be detached to take charge of the pack mules at once."

Cooke saluted with a flourish and spurred his magnificent white horse after the column. Reno looked a little uncertainly at General Terry and then, hesitantly, rendered another salute.

General Terry accepted his salute a little guiltily and stole a glance at a stony-faced Custer. Reno trotted off to join the fast-moving column, which was fording the wide but shallow Rosebud River, one company at a time.

Grasshopper Jim Brisbin turned away disdainfully as Custer warmly shook hands with Terry and Gibbon in turn. The commander of the 7th Cavalry in the field impatiently swung the head of his red sorrel around and started after the column.

"Don't be greedy, Custer," Gibbon said banteringly, "remember there are Indians enough for all of us."

"No, I w-won't," Custer answered seriously, and cantered away.

"Wait for us," Gibbon called after him.

The three reviewing officers walked their horses to the steamer *Far West* in silence. Dismounting, their reins taken by waiting orderlies, the three men stared at the column moving south by west in the distance.

"Well, Custer is happy now," General Terry remarked, "off on his own to scout for Indians."

Brisbin grunted noncommittally. Gibbon looked pale, probably as a result of a sick stomach that would have laid low a lesser man.

Terry misread his silence.

"You aren't a little envious, are you, John?" he asked with a gentle smile. "I mean, that Custer might get to the hostiles before the rest of us and capture all the glory?"

The hawklike infantry colonel nearly snorted. "Glory?" he asked as the three stopped at the end of the plank to the steamer. "Do you know what glory is out West? It's being shot by an Indian from behind a rock and having your name spelled wrong in the newspapers!"

General Terry laughed appreciatively. Even Grasshopper Jim twisted his face into a half sneer.

"You can depend on Custer to do what's best for himself," he said.

The three men watched the rising red dust as the long column moved along, crossed the Rosebud some two miles up, and pushed on. In a matter of minutes, the men and animals became black specks trailed by pillars of dust.

Custer hurried forward to catch a glimpse of the Indian and civilian scouts and guides moving quickly but carefully upstream. Lieutenant Varnum looked up from studying the ground before him and, as if summoned telepathically, trotted over beside Custer.

"The Crows are way up front," he reported. "The Rees are split. We're working both sides of the river. Bob-Tailed Bull has one detachment and Soldier has the other."

Custer nodded. "Where's my lucky man?"

Varnum looked puzzled for a minute and then answered, "Charlie Reynolds is on the left with Bull. I didn't post him. He just went."

"He knows," Custer said seriously. "The left flank is all-important. We can't afford to let them slip past us. Otherwise, this will be a wasted trip."

"We are going to switch from time to time," the pinch-faced chief of scouts went on. "Give us fresh eyes, so to speak."

Custer nodded absently. "Follow up every trail. The reds are devils when it comes to leaving false trails. Don't let them work around our left."

Varnum nodded and trotted forward. Custer rode to the top of a small rise and stood in his saddle, surveying his command. The companies were expertly echeloned so as to avoid one another's dust and not raise one large column of dust. The packtrain straggled badly. Custer frowned.

Moments later, he was joined by Lieutenant William W. Cooke, the adjutant. The two men didn't speak and Cooke's eyes followed Custer's around the horizon. He began scribbling in a small notebook.

Custer spoke at last. "We'll have to do something about those packs."

Cooke smiled, as though pleased with himself. "I've already made a note of it, General," he said. "I was thinking about detailing troops from each command to give the packers a hand."

Custer nodded. He walked his sorrel carefully down the hill to the trail and swung north, searching the horizon purposefully.

The column made good progress along the Rosebud River although they were strung out for at least two miles. The ground beneath the horses' hooves was sandy and almost devoid of vegetation, but was fairly level, except for the occasional dry ravines that ran into the shallow, fast-flowing Rosebud. Clumps of cottonwoods and wild roselike bushes grew in abundance close to the clear water. To the left of the column—the east geographically—irregular hills and mesas dotted the horizon. To the west, the ground rose sharply into the Wolf Mountains. It was not unlovely country.

The trumpeters had long since rejoined their companies, breaking up the parade massed-trumpets formation. There were two for each of the twelve companies: one attached himself to the company commander and the other to the first sergeant in the rear of each company. Chief Trumpeter Voss stuck to Custer and Lieutenant Cooke like glue.

They seemed to be moving away from the unseasonably cold weather of the Yellowstone. With each half mile, the sun peeped out further from behind disintegrating clouds and the air was warmer. Blue tunics and brown buckskin jackets were taken off and the column began to look gray rather than blue—as most of them sported the collarless gray flannel undershirt with its three-button placket front. Deerflies began to torment men and horses alike. Duty sergeants rode up and down the companies instructing men here and there to dismount and attend to saddlery. There were no stragglers, though, except for the mule train.

The 7th Cavalry went into camp about four-thirty in the afternoon after marching about twelve miles. The Rosebud was only three or four feet wide at the campsite and just inches deep. They camped at the base of a steep bluff close to the water and waited interminably for the lagging packs to arrive with their blankets and foodstuffs. They weren't idle in the meantime. Saddle girths were loosened and noncoms inspected the horses' skins under the blankets. If they were wet, the troopers were instructed to leave the saddles on a little longer; if they were dry, off came the saddles and the daily ritual began.

The saddles and bridles were wiped, the eyes of the horses were sponged, the heads and manes wisped, their feet inspected and picked. Finally, the horses, with saddles removed, were fed, watered, groomed, and lariated to fourteen-inch picket pins in the area designated to each company for picketing horses.

Fires were built, canteens were filled, and the precious, if monotonous, hardtack and meat were broken out. Coffee was boiled and those who did not choose to bathe in the shallow Rosebud filled their pipes or chewed their issue tobacco. Some of the enlisted men were called out for guard duty. Red-brassarded orderlies rode bareback up and down the length of the camp summoning the officers to an officers' call at Custer's bivouac.

The lucky enlisted men whose chores were done and who were not assigned guard duty skylarked generally with comrades. A few games of chance opened up and the newly paid cavalrymen, pockets laden with money, lined up to be parted with it to the mixed amusement and disgust of the others.

The sun, going down in the west behind dissipating storm clouds, covered the camp with a blood-red glow by the time all the officers had responded to the summons to headquarters. They seated themselves before a small cot—twenty-eight officers and three surgeons in all.

Adjutant Cooke and Lieutenant Colonel Custer were seated on the solitary cot, in front of which a small table had been erected. Custer leaned his elbows on the table and listened absently as Cooke read instructions from his notebook. The whiskered adjutant stroked his exceptional Dundrearies as he read in a monotone. There was to be no galloping, he read. Horses were not to be saddled until an hour before first light. This revelation brought a murmur from the assembly.

"No trumpets," Custer confirmed in his high-pitched, stammering voice. His eyes swept over his audience, not holding any glances. "We're in enemy country and we don't want our presence known until we are in a position to attack."

Another murmur greeted this remark. Custer flushed, but said nothing as Cooke droned on. Horses were to be brought inside the lines at sundown, sidelined, and securely picketed. Company commanders were responsible for security. On the march, no man was to be left behind. Company commanders were to take special measures to prevent straggling. The special measures were unspecified and a rumble punctuated by derisive laughter greeted this order. Custer glared around, but all the faces were blank when he jerked his head up. Cooke read on without a pause. After a few minutes more of routine instructions, he stopped abruptly. He looked expectantly at Custer.

Custer leaned forward, his voice lowered in earnestness.

"Marches will begin daily at five A.M. until further notice. All commands will be vocal. No shooting. No unnecessary noise. There will be no battalion or wing organizations."

His eyes swept his quiet audience, studiously ignoring dark-faced Major Reno—who flushed, but said nothing.

"Company commanders will be responsible directly to me," Custer went on. "You are all experienced and I am confident in the ability of each and every one of you. Hence, only two things will be dictated from regiment—when to move and where to camp for the night. We are rationed for fifteen days, but I expect to see action long before our rationing period draws to a close. All the other details—reveille, stables, watering, halting, and grazing— will be left to the discretion of the company commanders until further notice. Just keep within supporting distance of one another and don't get ahead of the scouts."

Custer seemed to be finished and, indeed, some of the seated men had shifted, preparatory to rising. The high-pitched, stammering voice stopped them. It was higher than before and a little more strident.

"I'm placing heavy reliance on the judgment and discretion of the unit commanders. And the loyalty." He glanced around sharply. "In the past, I have said little about the ceaseless grumbling from certain quarters. But we are now starting on a scout which we hope will be successful, and I intend to do everything in my power to make it as successful and pleasant as I can for everybody. I am certain that if any regiment in the service can do what is required of us, we can. I will be glad to listen to suggestions from any officer of the command, if made in the proper manner. But I want it distinctly understood that I shall allow no grumbling. I shall exact the strictest compliance with orders from everybody—not only with mine but with any order given by an officer to his subordinate. I don't want it said of this regiment as General Crook is supposed to have said of the 3rd Cavalry—that 'it would be a good one if he could only get rid of the old captains and let the young lieutenants command the companies.'"

A short bark of laughter greeted this, and stocky, white-haired Fred Benteen, the senior captain, shot to his feet, his clean-shaven face flushed and his large piercing blue eyes dancing.

"It seems to me, General," he rumbled, "that you are lashing the shoulders of all to get at some."

Benteen looked around the sea of faces with a tight smile on his face, seeming to relish the pin-prickling silence.

"Now, as we are all present," he went on, "would it not do to specify the officers whom you accuse?"

"I want the saddle to go where it fits," Custer snapped.

"Well, General," Benteen answered evenly, "I want a clear understanding. Am I accused of constant grumbling?"

Custer seemed to sigh and looked away almost wearily, but didn't answer.

"Are you charging Captain Keough here?" Benteen demanded. "Or Captain Weir?"

"Colonel Benteen," Custer said wearily at last, using the older man's Civil War rank as was customary, "I am not here to be catechized by you. But I will state publicly for your own information that none of my remarks have been directed at you."

Benteen sat down, his tight, humorless grin now somewhat puckish and he looked more jovial—like the "shaven Santa Claus" he was called behind his back.

It was an awkward minute before Custer found his voice again, and when he did, his voice was as unnaturally low as it had been at the outset. Heads jerked up at the sudden change.

"The number of hostiles who have persistently refused to live or enroll in the agencies is estimated at eight hundred to a thousand—these are the bucks only, naturally there are squaws and papooses. I would not be surprised to find there are fifteen hundred warriors out—though not all in the same place. We were offered some reinforcements from the 'lost tribes of the 2nd Cavalry.' I declined Major Brisbin's offer. After all, if the hostiles can whip the 7th, reinforcements would have little point. I left Mr. Lowe and his Gatling guns, because, being drawn by those condemned horses, they would only slow us down. Besides, as Gerard pointed out back on the steamer, we shouldn't allow ourselves to be de-

ceived into thinking the reds will stand still while we grind out
shots with a Gatling!"

Hearty laughter greeted this—heartier perhaps than the witti-
cism warranted. But it was the first good laugh the thirty-two men
had been able to squeeze into the very dour council.

"I tell you this," Custer went on with a half smile, "because I
want you to understand that this is strictly a 7th Cav affair. It's do
or die, this time, boys."

They cheered and Custer held up his hand.

"Husband your forces. Our marches will be twenty-five to thirty
miles a day until we make contact. After that . . . well, don't expect that we will let go." Custer faltered as he looked into the
eyes of each man in turn. His searching eye was met defiantly in
some cases and avoided sheepishly in others. Still others returned
his almost entreating glance with gazes of undisguised admiration.
Lastly, Custer looked at his adjutant, Cooke, who was scowling at
the notebook he held in his hand.

"The packs," Custer said in a musing tone of voice, "that
reminds me, gentlemen—our packtrain arrangement won't do.
The packers are working themselves into a frazzle trying to keep
the mules going and they are still not getting the job done. What
seems to be the problem, Major?"

Major Reno worked his heavy body into a crouching position
and leaned his elbows on his knees.

"It seems that the same packs are giving us trouble. They were
packed wrong to begin with. You see, balance is all-important—"

"Lieutenant Mathey," Custer broke in impatiently, addressing a
middle-aged lieutenant with side whiskers and large brown eyes,
"which packs are giving the most problems?"

"I'd really not . . . that is, I'd rather not name any company,
but some are worse than others as the major says, yes." First Lieutenant Edward G. "Gus" Mathey spoke with a heavy French accent. He had been put in charge of the packs at the Yellowstone.

Major Reno stood up. Coldly, he addressed the Frenchman.

"Lieutenant Mathey, which companies are giving the most
problems?"

"Well, sir," Mathey said hastily, "if I must choose, I would say
G Company and H Company—"

"E Company's not giving you any trouble, are they?" Lieutenant A. E. Smith cut in anxiously, rubbing his left arm absently.

Mathey ignored the stocky, cripple-armed commander of E Company as he saw Custer wave Smith to silence.

"So," Custer said briskly, "Lieutenant McIntosh and Captain Benteen have the worst records?"

"I wouldn't say it like that, General," Mathey protested weakly, rolling his eyes away from a red-faced Fred Benteen. Across the way, dark Tosh McIntosh was smiling good-naturedly with remarkably even white teeth.

The other officers exchanged uneasy glances and shifted uncertainly. Custer looked up almost absently.

"Dismissed," he stammered in his customary high-pitched voice.

The officers drifted away in groups of three or four toward their own respective units. Eaglelike Edward Godfrey of K Company was flanked by "Frank" Gibson, a square-faced, balding lieutenant with a heavy mustache from Benteen's H Company, and by Second Lieutenant George D. "Nick" Wallace. Nick Wallace, like Godfrey, was a West Pointer and was the tallest man in the regiment. He was a slender young man with a bony face, large nose, and receding chin. Immediately behind the trio was Frank Gibson's brother-in-law, Lieutenant Donald McIntosh, the part Indian who commanded G Company.

Nick Wallace slapped a white hat alongside his blue trousers and screwed his thin, homely face up into a frown. He leaned forward as if leaning into an imaginary wind.

"I believe General Custer is going to be killed," he said suddenly.

Godfrey looked first at Frank Gibson and then up at the gawky, blond-haired youngster on his other side.

"Why?" he asked. "What makes you think so, Wallace?"

"Because I have never heard him talk like that before."

Godfrey studied the earnest young man beside him like a bird of prey surveying his domain. At long last, he blinked—and the four men walked on in awed silence.

Second Lieutenant Winfield Scott Edgerly of D Company was one of a whole generation of young men named after the same famous general, but he, at least, had the distinction of resembling his namesake in physical build. Win Edgerly was thirty, an 1870 graduate of West Point, and a veteran of two campaigns on the frontier. He was the biggest man in the regiment (only Nick Wallace was taller) and certainly one of the handsomest. He stood six feet four, with broad shoulders and a large head that was covered with long, wavy dark hair carefully parted on the right side. A clipped mustache set off full, sensual lips and sparkling blue eyes above.

Seven other officers had been invited to his campfire after the officers' call for a songfest. That is to say, seven men besides Edgerly accepted and were present. It was an unusually large turnout for a group of officers that did not include Custer, but a sign of Edgerly's high regard that so many joined him. Tall, puffy-faced Major Reno was the senior man present.

The others were in a good mood to all appearances. Captain Myles Moylan with his sandy mustache and gun-barrel eyes represented A Company. Custer's handsome brother-in-law, Jim Calhoun—the company commander of L Company—was there representing the Custer family. First Lieutenant Frank Gibson had left Godfrey and his own brother-in-law, McIntosh, to join the party. "Gibby" was the practical joker of the regiment—a tall, slender, square-jawed man of twenty-eight, whose normal expression was that of a narrow-eyed owl. A. E. Smith, the chunky, cripple-armed commander of E Company, was also there.

A surgeon was there—Dr. Henry R. Porter. Dr. Porter had cultivated a drooping mustache to rival Ed Godfrey's, but his larger face and fine blond hair made it obvious that it would be months before the two hirsute embellishments could be fairly compared. The young man beside him didn't have that problem. Though only twenty-two years old, Second Lieutenant John Jordan Crittenden had a full light brown beard. He was a round-faced, cheerful-looking young man with a brown eye patch over his left eye. The eye had been put out by a freakish explosion of a rifle cartridge and young "J.J." Crittenden at first considered ending his Army career. But his father was a Civil War general and regimental commander with influence and J.J. had stayed on with the 20th Infantry. Custer had taken him along because the 7th Cavalry was chronically short of officers and even one-eyed infantry officers were useful, particularly those with political leverage. Crittenden was assigned to L Company and Jim Calhoun was responsible for his presence at the songfest.

Comradeship waxed as the evening waned. Lieutenant Calhoun's parting comment was like a benediction. He promised a piece of cake for each officer present. The cake was to be baked by his own wife, Margaret, Custer's younger sister, and to be consumed when the Indians had been found and beaten.

In the headquarters bivouac, George Armstrong Custer held court with his ubiquitous adjutant, Cooke, and his own two brothers and nephew. Also present were his old Civil War comrades-in-arms, Captains George Yates and Thomas B. Weir.

In addition to Captain Tom Custer, young Boston "Bos" Custer was along. Bos was a guide, having been a forager for the Department of Dakota since coming West for his health. A thin, consumptive man of twenty-five, he was clean-shaven and wore his reddish-blond hair long in the style made popular by his famous older brother. He was a civilian—as his appointment to second lieutenant in the 7th Cavalry had been delayed.

The nephew was Henry Armstrong Reed, an eighteen-year-old schoolboy on his first trip out West. "Autie" Reed was the oldest son of Custer's older half sister, Lydia, who had virtually raised the general as a young boy. Young Reed was rawboned like his famous uncle.

Homely Captain Weir of D Company was shaking his head in astonishment as Custer spoke rapidly to his audience.

"Captain Weir doesn't approve," Custer said laughingly.

Weir flushed and protested. "No, no. I just don't understand exactly what General Terry expects of us. Aren't we supposed to go all the way to the headwaters of the Tongue?"

Custer answered with a patronizing smile.

"As soon as we hit this trail Reno backed away from, we'll cut loose from Terry just like we did Stanley in '73 and bring in the hostiles ourselves."

"You're not going to scout the headwaters of the Tongue or the Rosebud?" George Yates wanted to know.

"I have a feeling Mr. Lo—the poor Indian—is just over there," Custer replied, waving his hand vaguely toward the west. "If our

scouts confirm this, there is no point in abandoning a fresh trail—
just because a staff officer wants to draw lines on a map."

"I didn't see this trail—" Weir began, but Tom Custer cut in.

"I did," the scar-faced commander of C Company said. "It's a
big one all right. The summer roamers from the agencies are joining the old holdouts, but this wasn't a summer group trail."

"The idea, Captain Weir," Cooke put in archly, "is to close
with Sitting Bull and his people before the agency bucks start
joining them in appreciable numbers."

"I know what the idea is, Cookey," Weir said sulkily.

"I'm worried," Custer said. "I'm afraid they may have held their
dances and split up to hunt the buffalo—which means they will
stay split up for the rest of the summer."

"What if the scouts don't locate the camp where you divine it
to be?" Yates asked.

Custer laughed shortly. "Then we can't proceed. You see, my
motto is: 'First be sure you're right, then go ahead.' If I am
proved right, however, I will charge the camp."

"Is it possible they'll give up without a fight?" Weir asked.

Custer nodded vigorously.

"It's possible," he conceded, "but I cannot plan a campaign re-
alistically unless I assume we'll have to fight."

He looked around at the faces watching him and frowned.

"I will make the proper decision at the proper time," he assured
them. "I am not impetuous or impulsive. I resent that. Everything
that I have ever done has been the result of the study that I have
made of imaginary military situations that might arise. Whenever
I became engaged in campaign or battle and a great emergency
arose, everything that I have ever read or studied focused in my
mind as if the situation were under a magnifying glass and my decision was the instantaneous result. My mind worked instan-
taneously, but always as a result of everything I had ever studied
being brought to bear on the situation."

"I'm sure the 7th will be glorified by your actions, General,"
Weir said pacifically.

Custer nodded and lapsed into a moody silence. Nothing further was said on the subject and conversation lagged.

Big-nosed Edward Godfrey walked upstream alone, lost in private thoughts. A burly half-breed wearing a leather vest over an agency calico shirt detached himself from the group of gesticulating Crows around a small fire and joined the K Company commander unseen. The half-breed scout was named Minton "Mitch" Bouyer, and he was well acquainted with the eastern Montana hunting grounds and, through his mother, the hostile Sioux in them.

"Lieutenant!" he called out gutturally. Godfrey whirled and instantly relaxed.

"Hello, uh—Bouyer, isn't it? Enjoying the dust-free night air?" Bouyer laughed and didn't answer. The two walked side by side along the gurgling stream without a word being exchanged between them for quite some distance. Bouyer kept glancing at the stern-looking Godfrey out of the corner of his eye. At last, seeming to be unable to contain himself any longer, he asked abruptly, "Have you ever fought against these Sioux?"

Godfrey turned and favored him with his unblinking eagle's stare.

"Yes," he answered matter-of-factly.

"Well, how many do you expect to find?"

Godfrey stopped walking. Slowly, quietly, he answered, "It is said we may find between eight hundred and a thousand warriors."

"Do you think you can whip that many?" Bouyer asked quickly.

Goddy was a long time in answering, but when he finally did, his voice was low and even. "Oh, yes, I guess so," he said.

Bouyer seemed confused by the answer and the tone of voice in which it was delivered. He was silent for a long time. Godfrey smiled patiently and turned to retrace his steps downstream. Bouyer spoke finally just as Godfrey began to move. His voice was thick with emotion.

"Well, I can tell you we are going to have a damned big fight!"

Godfrey stared unblinking at Mitch Bouyer and nodded solemnly. But he said nothing further and sauntered away when the scout dropped his hot gaze.

A short while later, Godfrey walked to a crude lean-to fashioned by a white canvas strip attached to the side of a larger than usual cottonwood not far from the river. He poked his head inside.

". . . and thees leetle boy, he kept toucheeng them weeth hees steecky hands . . ."

The audience laughed at the storyteller—a short, swarthy Italian named Charles C. DeRudio. First Lieutenant "Carlo" DeRudio was attached to A Company in place of A. E. Smith, who had gone to take command of DeRudio's old company, E—the Gray Horse Troop. DeRudio had white hair despite the fact that he was only forty-four years old, an imperial beard, and a long, waxed mustache. He wore a kepi tilted rakishly over his incongruous dark eyebrows.

". . . so thees leetle boy, he does eet one more time and I take hees steecky hands and I look at heem and I say, 'nice leetle boy, nice leetle boy,' and I craunch . . ."

Fred Benteen spit a pipestem out of his mouth and chuckled—a merry sound that carried almost across the river. Captain Myles Keough was the only other listener and he leaned against the tree the canvas was fastened to, his dark hat pulled down low over his eyes. Even in the dark, his teeth flashed.

"Welcome to the church service," pipe-puffing Benteen boomed genially from his position—cross-legged on the ground with his boots removed and standing free beside him.

Keough lifted his dark hat, saw that the newcomer was Godfrey, and lowered it again.

"Carlo doesn't know how to use his hands," he explained. "He's forever putting something in them he shouldn't have, you know."

DeRudio laughed easily. "Like that saber I took from those nice people in Kansas. GAC was furioso."

He pronounced Custer's initials "Jack," the popular nickname of the blond cavalry commander.

"What was that last word?" Benteen asked mock-seriously.

"You didn't drag a great bloody saber along with you, did you, old man?" Keough bantered.

DeRudio laughed and addressed a stony-faced Godfrey. "Mathey has one heeden een the packs where he can't get to eet."

"I've just had a talk with one of our scouts," Godfrey said abruptly. "He seems to feel we are in for the fight of our lives."

"Ah, but we'll have to catch the heathen first," Keough said softly in his thick Irish brogue.

"They'll run us ragged," Benteen said confidently, "but as to a fight—I don't know. We've got twelve companies of cavalry and more than twenty-five thousand rounds of ammunition."

He paused almost pensively.

"I wish they would stand and fight for a change," he went on, more seriously. "We could end this business in a few hours and get back to our station. If they fight, it will be a short campaign."

"How many Sioux are there?" DeRudio wanted to know.

"You heard GAC," Benteen told him. "Eight hundred to a thousand, maybe as many as fifteen hundred."

"Altogether, I mean," the little Italian pressed. "Fifty thousand?"

"Something like that," Keough admitted, "but you don't expect to find that many out there, do you?"

"What difference does it make?" Benteen argued, grinning. "They'll run and that's a fact. Fifty or fifty thousand—it makes no difference."

"You don't really believe that yourself, old man," Keough said quietly.

Godfrey broke the sudden somber silence.

"The marksmanship of the regiment is the worst I've known it since I joined. I wish we had spent more time firing at targets. We could even have selected a group of marksmen like we did before the Washita."

There was an incoherent growl from Benteen inside the lean-to. Keough laughed.

"What are you trying to do, Goddy? Would you wave a red cape in front of a bull?"

"My point was—" Godfrey began.

"Washita!" Benteen's voice came out coherently in a roar at last. "Washita!"

"What happened at the Washita, Fred?" Keough asked mock-innocently.

There was an awkward silence as the normally genial Benteen recovered. When he spoke, he was smiling with his lips, but not his eyes.

"At the Washita," he said in a near-reverent whisper, "we lost Major Elliott, Sergeant Major Kennedy—a fine young soldier—

and sixteen enlisted men and damn me if any search was made for them until a fortnight later."

Hefty Captain Tom McDougall arrived on the scene. He bustled past Godfrey and took a seat on the ground between DeRudio and Benteen.

"What did I miss?" he wheezed.

"Some disloyal slanderin'," Keough put in drily, "grumblin' constantly, I believe it's called."

McDougall looked from a silent Benteen to a silent Godfrey to a grinning Keough.

"Uh-oh," he murmured, "the Washita."

Keough burst out laughing. Benteen smiled and even Godfrey grinned.

"Well," McDougall said, "you've got the packtrain escort tomorrow, Fred. Wages of sin, I guess."

"How did you come to know thees eentelligence?" DeRudio demanded.

"I got it straight from the horse's mouth."

"GAC?" Benteen asked, astonished.

"Mathey," McDougall answered after a second's pause, which he appeared to enjoy immensely.

"The horse's mouth, eh?" Benteen rumbled. "The horse's ass, more likely."

Keough almost fell down laughing and even Godfrey was chuckling in an awkward way.

"What have I done, O Lord?" Benteen asked. "Mosquitoes by night, no sleep. Mathey by day, and no sense. Why me?"

They all laughed.

Friday, June 23, 1876

It was still dark when the column pulled out. The order of march looked pretty much the same as the day before except that crusty old Fred Benteen was responsible for the security of the 160 mules and extra horses in the packtrain. The three companies under his command trotted, then walked, and all too often halted as the packtrain ahead of them made its way by fits and starts south and now a little east as the Rosebud meandered to within ten miles of the Tongue River.

The scouts were far out in front—lost to sight. They trotted ahead confidently, now and again sweeping from side to side. The most remarkable feature to their maneuverings was that they appeared to pay little attention to the ground. They rode, for the most part, with their eyes on the horizon in front of them, on all sides of them, and, occasionally, behind them.

The scouts signaled that the trail crossed the narrow, winding Rosebud and they themselves crossed at a natural ford where the little river coursed around a sudden bend caused by the heavy line of broken bluffs to the west. At the ford site, the Rosebud ran east-west and, without hesitation, the cavalry crossed the river. The packs were exceptionally difficult to manage and Benteen's expression was far from angelic as he none too patiently supervised the crossing, while the three companies under his command waited stoically on the north side. It took the 160 pack mules and spare horses an hour and a half to cross the Rosebud, which was eighty feet wide at that point.

The packs crossed the Rosebud five times in the incredibly short distance of three miles and, while they improved efficiency with each crossing, they were scattered for two miles by nine o'clock in the morning.

Lieutenant Nick Wallace, the "Long Soldier" of the regiment, consulted his watch and recorded that it was 9 A.M. when the scouts found the trail. Wallace was the engineer officer and responsible for the itinerary. The trail came to the Rosebud from the east and followed south along its east bank toward the headwaters.

Three miles ahead of the packs, Custer was in conference with a half dozen scouts, including Lieutenant Varnum and Mitch Bouyer. Bloody Knife, a part Sioux, part Ree, who was a guide rather than a scout, had just halved a horse apple with his knife and looked up, holding his fingers inches apart. His solemn face had no expression as he wiped the knife in the grass. A red flannel band held his long gray hair away from his face and he wore a plaid shirt and buckskin trousers above knee-length moccasins. He rumbled gutturally in Ree. Custer turned inquiringly to Fred Gerard, a tall, rangy, black-eyed man in his forties.

"A week," Gerard translated carelessly in his sharp, overly loud voice. "Maybe ten days."

Gerard was dressed plainly, almost severely, in dark blue government issue cast-offs and wore a pair of knee-length, fancily beaded moccasins similar to Bloody Knife's. Gerard was an educated man who had inexplicably made his life on the plains of the Dakotas as a fur trader and squaw man. Later, he had been appointed post translator at Fort Lincoln. Despite his years of experience with Indians, this was his first expedition with the 7th Cavalry.

Custer nodded thoughtfully. Mitch Bouyer insisted there was a large village ahead.

"Show me," Custer stammered.

At the tail of the column, a sharp-eyed duty sergeant chivying stragglers called out a warning. Benteen pulled off the trail and called for Lieutenant DeRudio, who was watering his own horse in the river while ostensibly keeping the mules away from the water. The little Italian dandy trotted over.

"Let me see those fancy glasses " Benteen growled.

DeRudio fumbled in his saddlebag and within seconds produced a pair of Austrian field glasses of exceptionally fine resolution. Benteen fiddled with them incessantly, studying the horizon to the south intently.

"What is it?" pale-faced Dr. George Lord, the senior surgeon, demanded. First Lieutenant Lord was a slight, straight-backed man with glasses and a long mustache.

Benteen cocked a worried eye up and down the column. He stared at the hopelessly disordered packtrain and the three companies behind it. He searched the terrain to his right—the west—and scowled. Looking south again, he saw that the nearest company in front was out of sight. The mules were all over the valley.

"This won't do," he thought out loud.

DeRudio looked perplexed as Benteen absently returned the binoculars.

"Not only are we eating mule dust with no relief, but there is no security in it," the white-haired senior captain explained. "Not to mention sense."

Benteen stared grimly at Dr. Lord, DeRudio, Gibson, and the score of soldiers who had halted around him and who were pointing south.

"Indian sign," he informed all within earshot. "This won't do," he repeated.

Suddenly, the company immediately before the mule train came into view—deployed. Benteen galloped forward with his red face suddenly white.

"What is it?" he called to the first officer he saw.

A grizzled sergeant answered tensely. "Indian sign."

Benteen looked back at the packtrain and the trailing three companies with a look of annoyance. He trotted back through the packs in grim silence. When he arrived back at the little congregation he had left, his eyes brightened with sudden decisiveness. He beckoned a swarthy, flat-nosed trumpeter. Private John Martin appeared beside him.

"Tell Lieutenant Mathey to halt the packtrain," Benteen growled. He stared at the perplexed young Italian immigrant trumpeter and repeated slowly in careful English: "Lieutenant Mathey. To halt mules. Go on."

Martin galloped. Minutes later, the mules were halted.

Benteen huddled with several officers and noncoms and rapped out a stream of orders in a tone that brooked no argument. It took nearly a half hour for the exasperated sergeants to form the sweating, cursing troopers and their recalcitrant mounts into the positions dictated—but when they finished, only one company was actually behind the mules. One company was echeloned on the right, or western, flank. The third company was strung out in front of the packtrain, closing the gap between the mules and the rest of the column. Arranged like this, they made only slightly faster progress, but they were all together and Benteen's expression seemed to indicate that he was pleased with the new arrangement.

The sun rose scorchingly hot and the column walked on. The companies stopped frequently—but by themselves. Only Benteen and his three-company packtrain guard remained together— bunched uncomfortably, but securely, close.

The trail wasn't all that much at first, but with each advancing half mile it seemed to grow. Pony tracks and droppings in the sparse sandy soil were joined by narrow ruts caused by pine poles dragged travois-style behind yet more ponies. Occasionally, a scout would wave a strip of tanned buffalo hide or a bone or wooden object tossed off by the Indians who had made the trail.

On the other side of the Rosebud, Custer was in conference with his scouts. The remains of a large camp could be plainly seen. The discolored circular patches on the ground marked the locations of Indian lodges.

Bouyer explained the markings left by the Indians. He pointed out a strange pile of sand with sticks pointed toward the west and leaning.

"Lakota is confident," he grunted. "These are soldiers falling into the Indian camp upside down. It means they will fight and they are confident they will win."

Custer seemed not to hear. Making sure Gerard was listening, he addressed Bloody Knife.

"Is this the trail you found for Major Reno?"

Gerard translated and Bloody Knife nodded emphatically. He spoke urgently in Ree.

"He says there are many," Gerard translated in his loud, grating voice. "Many more than he has ever seen together at one time."

"That's the information we have from General Sheridan," Custer agreed coolly, "but they'll run from the 7th."

The column moved ahead at a walk. Custer rode beside Varnum.

"Here is where Reno made the biggest mistake of his life," Custer said. "He had six companies and enough rations for a number of days. He'd have made a name for himself if he'd pushed on after them."

"Well, General," Varnum remarked, "it seems that it will fall to you to add more luster to your own name."

Custer chuckled reflexively and then, after a moment's reflection, sobered.

"In the past," he said quietly, "my every thought was ambitious. Not to be wealthy, not to be learned—but to be great. I desired to link my name with acts and men and in such a manner as to be a mark of honor not only to the present but to future generations."

The two men rode on in strained silence as Custer seemed to be in deep thought and Varnum in uncomfortable anticipation.

"My ambition has been turned into an entirely new channel," Custer concluded in his rapid-fire voice, his pale blue eyes flashing with fervor. "Where once I was eager to acquire worldly honors and distinctions, I am content to try and modestly wear what I have and feel grateful for them when they come. My desire is to make myself worthy of the blessings heaped on me."

He looked into the pinched face of his chief of scouts and turned away abruptly. Varnum opened his mouth to say something, then closed it as Custer cantered away.

Benteen's first lieutenant, Frank Gibson, rode beside Lieutenant Mathey, the packtrain commander.

"Have you heard from your lovely little wife?" the Frenchman asked Gib by way of conversation.

"Yes," replied the mustachioed prankster. "Fort Rice is different without the cavalry and, in another sense, it's the same."

"What a miserable place," Mathey agreed.

"She told me about the time you found her working late in the night and escorted her over to the Benteens'. You found some tacks for a coffin she was making, I guess."

"Jesus, yes," Mathey breathed. "I remember. The women were burying Benteen's little girl and I didn't know anything about it. I was duty officer that night, and as I passed by your quarters, I saw the lights still on. This was well past midnight, as I recall. She was in tears and I asked her what the matter was."

Mathey spit into the sandy soil and continued with a hushed voice. "She was lining an ammunition crate with pieces of her wedding dress for a coffin. I found some tacks with white heads that matched the material and took her and the box over to the Benteens'. You were in the field and so was Colonel Benteen."

Gibson nodded. "How many children has Mrs. Benteen lost now? Three or four?"

"Three that I know of," Mathey answered. "Only the boy, little Freddy, lived."

"A chip off the old block, eh, Mathey?"

Mathey smiled. "He wants to be a cowboy."

"He'll be a soldier. The old man won't have anything less."

"Poor boy," Mathey murmured. And the two men rode on with little to say.

Altogether, the cavalry found three abandoned campsites. Bouyer became glum when Custer cold-shouldered him. Custer rode with Lonesome Charlie Reynolds, a stocky guide with a high forehead and piercing blue eyes. Reynolds' right arm was in a sling due to an infected index finger.

"I understand you went to General Terry and asked to be relieved," Custer remarked frostily.

"My hand is giving me a lot of pain," the quiet little scout replied. "Besides, Bouyer and the Crows know the country better than anyone. And you've got that young cowboy, George Herendeen, now. I figured you wouldn't need me."

"I hope you don't feel left out," Custer remarked after a painful pause.

"No, General. I just thought I wouldn't be needed as a scout or messenger—you've got the nigger Isaiah for that. I can't shoot without a lot of pain and I can't shoot straight at all. I figured I'd just be an extra mouth to feed and an extra horse that could better be used elsewhere."

"I still have work for you," Custer said.

The two men rode side by side in awkward silence.

"Charlie," Custer finally asked, "what do you think of all this?

What will the Indians do? Where will they go? We haven't heard your views yet."

"General," replied Reynolds quietly, "if you were an Indian, what would you do?"

"If I were an Indian," Custer answered seriously, "I would greatly prefer to cast my lot among those people who adhered to the free open plains rather than submit to the confined limits of a reservation."

Reynolds' wide face held no expression.

"Would you fight?" he asked.

"I would fight," Custer said decisively.

It was late afternoon when the column halted and went methodically into camp. Horses were unsaddled, rubbed, and securely picketed after rolling in the grass for fifteen minutes. The farriers checked hooves assiduously. The men not on duty lounged in the grass in small groups and some betook themselves to the water as they had the night before, but the gaiety and horseplay were subdued.

The packs were almost two hours behind the rest, and Lieutenant Cooke, stroking his whiskers and bantering with Captain Keough, greeted Benteen and the other company commanders, pointing out bivouac sites. There was the usual hubbub as representatives from each of the twelve companies sought out the mules with their own respective company's gear.

"See here, Cookey," Benteen boomed jocularly, "GAC ordered me to march the three troops composing the packtrain guard in the *rear* of the last mule."

"Yes, sir, I know that," Cooke replied stiffly.

Benteen smiled thinly. "Now, as he told us last night that he was open for recommendations, et cetera, I tell you as adjutant of the regiment that the first thing we know some casabianca will be getting the same such orders about the train." He lowered his voice seriously. "And if the roughness of the country holds out and the Indian signs continue to thicken, why, the trains will go up."

Cooke regarded him stonily.

"Then," the senior captain concluded heavily, "the circus adjourns."

Cooke walked his fine white horse alongside Benteen's long-legged bay for some distance in awkward silence.

"Can't you slip in a mention of my new arrangement when the general is in a receptive mood?" Benteen asked.

"If you have a recommendation for the general," Cooke answered frostily, "you'd be advised to bring it to him yourself. After last night, I wouldn't think he would be too receptive to actions that flaunt his expressed orders."

The tall adjutant trotted away without a backward glance.

Major Reno encountered an unsmiling Fred Benteen.

"What is it?" he asked.

Benteen told him. Reno jerked his head contemptuously.

"Cookey's one of those damned foreign adventurers who have cluttered up the Army List since the war. It's a cross we have to bear."

"That damned coffee cooler," Benteen growled, and then suddenly his face lit up in a mischievous grin. "But he can sure play politics, can't he?"

Reno nodded cautiously, not speaking.

"He was my second-in-command right after the Washita," Benteen related brittlely. "As a result of my 'chick' on the Washita which a friend had printed in a newspaper without my knowledge, GAC assigned me to Fort Dodge. My wife was sick at Harker and my little girl dead and unburied, but Dodgewards I went. Cookey got himself a leave and transferred to I Company without a backward glance." He laughed harshly. "Well, when the Inspector General divined what had happened, I was relieved of Dodge in a trice. Cookey was leading Custer's escort for General Marcy when next I saw him. I was in a ditch cutting the throat of a buffalo cow I had shot.

" 'Up to your old trade, I see,' he says.

" 'Yes,' I told him, 'I can't keep out of blood.' "

Benteen laughed heartily at the reminiscence. "Off he rode without so much as a nod. We haven't had a good word for each other since. Of course, he showed the white feather at the Washita. The troops know his full measure."

Reno groaned. "The Washita, the Washita. Must we keep fighting it over and over?"

Benteen and Keough skylarked—that is, drank coffee, smoked, and gossiped—all night. They were joined at the outset by Keough's former opponent in the Italian Civil War, DeRudio, and later by the roly-poly commander of B Company, Captain Tom McDougall. Flat-faced Captain French of M Company joined them briefly for a discussion of tactics.

"All this lines and angles stuff is nonsense to me," he declared in his gin-husky voice, his black eyes glittering in the light of the small coffee-pot fire. "Ask me, there's too many Napoleons running around once the shooting starts. When I was in the 10th during the war, it seemed we had more people running around outside the formation telling us to keep dressed right than were actually in the ranks doing the job."

"You can't complain about that in the 7th," Keough observed.

French nodded. "GAC's a man after my own heart. None of your senseless orders. Just 'Follow me, men.' "

Benteen spoke up. "I always find it better to give suggestions rather than orders. After all, most grown men don't have to be told how to fight."

"Exactly," French said, a little unclearly. "There's only one rule in fighting—that's the old rule of Donnybrook Fair: 'If you see a head, hit it'—simple."

DeRudio was a little dubious. "Eet would help to know where we go and why."

"What's wrong with: 'There's the enemy'?" French demanded.

"It seems to me I've heard that expression before," McDougall put in.

"Balaclava," Keough supplied, "the Charge of the Light Brigade."

"Well, we don't have to worry about charging cannon where we're going," Benteen decided. "It'll be mostly trot, trot, trot, and once in a while shoot at a feather sticking up behind a rock."

"These Indians are poor shots," French declared.

"Don't you believe it," Benteen told him.

Benny Hodgson, Captain McDougall's second lieutenant, had attached himself to Major Reno. Hodgson was normally Reno's adjutant when Reno had a command and they socialized naturally from force of habit. Benjamin Hubert Hodgson was a small, very erect man with bright eyes and a bushy mustache. He was twenty-eight, a classmate of big Win Edgerly's at West Point. The troops called him the "Jack of Clubs" and his fondness for excitement and adventure had nearly brought him to grief the previous winter. He had tendered his resignation from the Army and only news of the campaign had prompted him to withdraw it.

Hodgson and Reno were listening to the tales of the Fort Lincoln interpreter and poultry farmer, Fred F. Gerard.

"It was just a few years after the war," the civilian plainsman was saying in his too loud voice, "1868, I believe. It was over a bunch of Iroquois shells. Old Sitting Bull was pulling his strong-arm tactics as usual. He figured he had all those wild ones to back him up and he'd show up a yellow eye like me. Well—" He laughed shortly, a sharp bark. "I grabbed his greasy hand and took them right back. Pulled a gun on me, the son of a bitch. One of my Ree friends stepped in and we took it away from him."

"Why didn't you kill him?" Reno wanted to know. "Save all this trouble."

"I'd have started all this 'trouble,' as you call it. He had fifty bucks on the other side of the river."

Hodgson laughed delightedly and leaned forward, his large eyes shining.

"That wasn't the end of it," Gerard went on. "He sent word through Bloody Knife that he had an arrow in his quiver for me."

Reno looked startled. "He did what?"

"That's right," Gerard confirmed, seeming to relish the suspense. "I sent word back to him that I had a rifle that spoke true and if he ever came back, he would hear it speak."

Hodgson whistled in admiration.

"He's steered clear of you since then, hasn't he?"

"Until now," Gerard admitted. "I don't like the idea of us finishing things. Especially when he has upwards of fifteen hundred bucks behind him."

"That's okay, Mr. Gerard," Hodgson assured him, "you have Custer's 7th Cavalry behind you."

"That ought to be something to see," Reno remarked quietly, as the three men laughed appreciatively.

"Yeah," Gerard added wistfully, "for a while there, I thought it was going to be Reno's 7th Cavalry."

Reno flushed and said nothing.

"It might be yet," Benny Hodgson murmured loyally.

Reno clapped the younger man silently on the shoulder.

"What's he like?" Reno asked Gerard, after a long silence. "Sitting Bull, I mean. What does he look like?"

"Oh," Gerard answered slowly, "he's tall for a Sioux. Well built. Not a bad-looking chap. Dirty, though—and two-tongued. Full of the devil."

"He's not much of a fighter, I gather," Hodgson prompted.

"He's a talker, a rabble rouser." Gerard seemed lost in thought for a minute. "You see, when an Indian gets to be my age—or his age—they're not expected to fight. They let the young bucks do the fighting and they sit around making medicine."

"Not a bad idea," Reno said wearily. "For my own part, I'm sick of fighting. I wish I knew something else—something commercial. I think I'd like to be in business for myself—have regular hours, a warm bed, full table, and be able to see my son grow up."

Saturday, June 24, 1876

Custer was one of the first to stir before dawn. On his way to the river, he was hailed by Fred Benteen, bleary-eyed from a lack of sleep for the second night in a row. Benteen very matter-of-factly told Custer of the new pack-escort formation.

Custer nodded emphatically as he listened to Benteen's explanation.

"I am grateful to you, Colonel Benteen," he said, "and I will turn over the same order of march for the rear guard to the officer who relieves you."

"Captain Yates, you mean, General," the white-haired H Company commander said. "He knows all about the arrangement. And since all it really needed was your blessing, why, bring 'em on."

Custer smiled wanly. "I hope you didn't regard the pack assignment as a punishment detail. I put you on it first because I wanted the details to be in fine tune and didn't have time to tend to them myself. I knew I could depend on you to find the best way."

With that, he walked away, leaving his senior captain to stare after him in suspicious amazement.

The column was on the trail by the first light that peeped over the jagged hills to the east. They moved briskly at a fast walk, but the horses tired sooner than on the previous two days and, within hours, the pace had slowed down. Deerflies and almost microscopic buffalo gnats plagued the horses as well as the men. The insects seemed to be concentrated in the shade of the rather skimpy cottonwoods along the shallow Rosebud. They swarmed into eyes and bored into ears without regard to rank or position.

Godfrey may not have been the first to notice it, but he was the one who called it to Custer's attention. He was shaking his head

violently to ward off a particularly persistent insect when he happened to see puffs rising from the tops of the low, irregular Wolf
Mountains—far to the right—or west.

"Smoke signals," pronounced a young trooper just recently
joined, though he had probably never seen a smoke signal before
in his life.

Custer, a half mile ahead of the rest of the column with a two-
company escort, consulted the scouts after courteously thanking
Godfrey for the intelligence. Lieutenant Varnum didn't see them
well, but two of the sharp-eyed Crows assured Mitch Bouyer that
they were only clouds. The burly half-breed passed on the information to Custer in the presence of an obviously annoyed
Varnum.

"I don't see anything," the pinch-faced chief of scouts insisted.
"How can you be sure?"

"They don't *say* anything," Bouyer replied briefly, and trotted
away.

Custer laughed at the crestfallen expression on Varnum's face.
"You're learning," he approved. "These scouts are inclined to see
hostiles behind every rock. If they say it is nothing, chances are
there is nothing. But be alert."

Varnum moved ahead unhappily, glancing warily at the smoke
in the distance.

"They've spotted us," Captain George Yates told his young
lieutenant, William van Wyck Reily. Yates was a thickset, blond-
bearded man with a large nose and a fringed buckskin shirt that
was obviously too warm. His parade-smart F Company, now ragged, dusty scarecrows, rode among the pack mules as part of the
escort. Reily was a darkly handsome man of twenty-two and a
half with a narrow face and a strikingly square jaw. He had been
appointed a second lieutenant less than a year before—straight
from civilian life—although he had spent two years at the Naval
Academy (Annapolis) before resigning. He was dark: dark-
skinned, dark-haired, and dark-eyed in sharp contrast to Yates's
Teutonic fairness. He tugged at the front of his sweat-stained blue
shirt and waved away a swarm of buffalo gnats. He swept off his
trader-bought straw hat and revealed his low-set ears, dark eyebrows, and heavy black mustache.

"Maybe they're clouds," he answered, apparently unwilling to open his mouth any more than was absolutely necessary because of the bugs. His thin, hooked nose flared. "We ought to send a party of scouts over that direction to check—"

"General Custer knows what he is doing," Yates rumbled placidly. "Our only concerns are F Company and the packs. That's the trouble with this regiment—there are too many regimental commanders."

"I guess it all boils down to whether or not we trust GAC," Reily said.

Yates looked surprised. "We have no choice. He is in command."

Near the head of the column, George Herendeen trotted up beside Custer in response to the general's signal. Custer removed his large-brimmed white hat and nodded coolly at the young cowboy from Montana. He used the large white hat as a fan to drive away a swarm of insects.

Herendeen was average-looking with a small mustache that was fashionable and close-cropped hair—which made him identical in appearance to most of the twenty-eight officers and three surgeons that accompanied the expedition. In fact, were it not for his civilian attire, he might have been mistaken for an officer. His shirt and general bearing made him appear different. He took no interest in the column—in the struggling troopers trying desperately to control irritated and green horses and wandering all over the valley in the process. Herendeen kept his borrowed cavalry mount well in hand and paid no attention to march distance or interval.

The young guide eyed the temporarily hatless Custer diffidently. Custer's famous yellow locks were nowhere in evidence. His hair was close-cropped and his drooping mustache was complemented by a stubbly reddish beard. His buckskin jacket was open and flapped as he nudged his horse ahead to get away from the gnats. Herendeen kept up with him. At length, Custer replaced his hat.

"Tulloch Creek is just over there, isn't it?" Custer asked as he gestured toward the puffs of mist.

Herendeen nodded.

"I'm thinking I should send you and Reynolds and maybe a

couple troopers down the headwaters to report to Terry as we were instructed. Now's the time, don't you think?"

"Well, General," replied the young cowboy quietly, "there's a pass just up ahead that isn't but about fifteen minutes' ride from the headwaters. It leads up into a sort of divide, and if it is all the same to you, I think we should stay with the column until we come to that pass. The ground over to the right is too rough and we'd have to stick to the trail anyway."

Custer nodded. "You're right," he said. "You might as well stay with us a little while longer."

Herendeen was about to move away when a sudden gesture from Custer stayed him. "Could the Indians have gone over this divide?" Custer asked.

Herendeen was a long time in answering. "Why, yes, General," he said slowly at last, "I reckon they could have."

Custer nodded and gestured for Cooke to join him. Herendeen waited and, seeing the conference didn't include him, trotted away.

The column recrossed the Rosebud at noon. The overhead sun was scorching and, as on the day before, the troops removed their wool tunics and rode nonchalantly in their gray flannel collarless undershirts. Those officers affecting the plainsman look with buckskin jackets sensibly removed them and displayed variously designed blue flannel shirts. Most were the pullover "fireman's" shirt with its panel and double row of buttons. Custer set the trend in that regard, wearing a cleverly sewn paneled pullover with yellow tape and mother-of-pearl buttons—a monument to the domestic craftsmanship of Mrs. Custer. It had a wide, falling collar and was open at the throat. It looked cool as well as comfortable.

Tom Custer and A. E. Smith were similarly favored with handmade shirts of excellent workmanship. Some of the officers were not so fortunate—having neither loving nor skillful wives. They wore the blue wool tunic stoically. Major Reno was one of them.

He plucked his tunic away from his perspiring body for the thirtieth time in as many minutes and looked crossly at red-eyed Fred Benteen, who swayed in the saddle alongside him.

"Where are we going?" he demanded. "Does anyone know?"

Benteen mumbled something unintelligible.

Reno mopped his brow. "GAC told Varnum I wasn't fit to command," he said.

Benteen looked at Reno with renewed interest, an easy grin never faltering.

"Well," he drawled, "ain't that a case of the pot calling the kettle black?"

Reno nodded glumly. "I knew Custer during the war and I have no confidence in his leadership."

"Stand up to him," Benteen counseled. "The rest of the officers in this regiment are like so much cattle, but you won't find the boy general running roughshod over me. He knows I'll stand up to him."

"He seems to like you for it," Reno agreed.

"I've always felt that Custer likes me and that he wants me badly for a friend," Benteen said musingly, and then, shaking his massive white head, dourly added, "but we can never be."

"Because of the Washita?"

"That was the straw that broke the camel's back," Benteen conceded. "Joel Elliott was a captain in my brigade during the war. A finer young man you'll never know. GAC *told* him to pursue those Indians with orders to 'let none get away.' He heard the shooting all morning. Godfrey reported it to him twice, but no search was made and Joel Elliott and seventeen troopers were hacked to pieces by the Cheyenne within supporting distance of eleven companies of cavalry armed with repeating carbines."

"That's not the way Custer tells it," Reno said mildly.

Benteen jerked his hand in a gesture of contempt and didn't expand verbally.

"Well, if there's one thing I have learned," Reno said finally, "it is that it doesn't pay to kick against the pricks. You can't fight men like Custer. You only lose."

Benteen snorted. "I've been a loser, in a way, all my life by rubbing against the angles—or fur—of folks, instead of going with their whims; but I couldn't go otherwise—'twould be against the grain of myself."

Varnum came trotting back in response to Custer's summons an hour after the column had crossed the Rosebud. He found the general inspecting the large Sun Dance lodge that was still standing. There were two officers besides Lieutenant Cooke with him. Varnum recognized Godfrey and Second Lieutenant Luther Rector Hare, both of K Company. Custer was livid.

"The first thing I told you when we began this scout," he stammered at Varnum, "was to follow up every trail. Lieutenant Godfrey here found a trail about ten miles back leading to the left —the *left*, Mr. Varnum. Do you know what that means?"

"Yessir," Varnum replied stiffly, wearily.

"How could you miss it? Are you relying too much on these Crows?"

"General," Varnum answered, raising his voice to match Custer's, "I've had the half-breeds and Gerard in front all the way up the river. I can't believe they would let anything get past them. If they passed it up, it is because it joins the main trail a little further on. Reynolds is supervising the left. I can't believe he'd miss it."

Custer's voice was strangely hoarse. "Well, obviously the unbelievable has happened. Check it out, Mr. Varnum, check it out personally. We'll have to hold up the entire column until you've rectified your mistake."

"General—"

"Mr. Varnum," Custer shouted him down, as the others moved discreetly away, "when I told you two days ago to check out all trails—especially to the left—that was an order! Do you need to be reminded about our policies with regards to orders in the 7th Cavalry?"

"Yes, sir. I mean, no, sir. I'll take some of the Rees and we'll check it out personally."

"Lieutenant Godfrey will show you the way. I'm detaching Mr. Hare to use as your assistant in the meantime." Custer's voice was crisp and sharp still, but the edge was gone. He smiled. "You can use the help. You've got a big responsibility and you're tired. These things happen."

"It won't happen again, General," Varnum assured him grimly.

Custer nodded and walked over to where Lieutenant Hare stood holding the reins of his own horse and Dandy, the general's mount.

Hare was a tall, thin Texan with abnormally broad shoulders,

who had graduated from West Point only two years before. He
was clean-shaven with high cheekbones and close-set dark eyes. He
wore his blue uniform as carelessly as a cattle-driving cowboy,
which he resembled.

"When Mr. Varnum comes back," Custer told Hare, "I want
you to take the right flank to give him the opportunity to concentrate on our left. If the trail crosses the divide ahead, I want to be
sure we stay on it."

Varnum was talking in low, curt tones to Godfrey as the Rees
came up.

"Take Mr. Hare's horse," Custer called to his frustrated chief
of scouts, "yours looks like he could use a rest."

Custer mounted expertly and, trailed by a solemn-looking adjutant, Cooke, cantered downstream toward the column. Varnum
followed, mounted on Hare's horse. Eagle-beaked Godfrey rode
beside him, carefully avoiding his glare.

Varnum found that the missed trail had indeed returned to the
main trail, but it was a good three hours before he was able to report this fact to an increasingly restless Custer. Almost simultaneously, Gerard led another group of scouts back. They were
excited and Gerard's translation merely confirmed what their
demeanor advertised.

"More pony tracks," the loud interpreter rapped out. "Ten
miles further up. They cross the divide all right. Big trail. Biggest
I've ever seen and not more than two days old."

Bouyer nodded enthusiastically and added comments of his
own that were inaudible in the general excitement.

Custer looked outwardly calm. Turning to Lieutenant Cooke,
he instructed: "Assemble the commanders. Use gallopers. No
trumpets."

His voice betrayed his excitement. Cooke trotted away to do his
bidding.

Finally, Bouyer's voice could be heard.

"General, there's an old lookout on the divide about fifteen
miles from here. Crows use it for hunting and spying out the land.
You can see the valley of the Little Big Horn from there on a
clear day."

Custer looked at the big blue sky with an almost rapturous look.

The scouts gathered around Custer as he waited for the officers to assemble. They murmured together in their own languages—mostly Ree. One of them, an older man named Stabbed, began to harangue the younger members and almost spontaneously began to demonstrate the way they should avoid the Sioux while getting within striking distance of the pony herd.

Custer laughed appreciatively and patted the old Indian on the shoulder.

"Yes, Stabbed," he told the Rees and their demonstrator through Gerard, "you scouts are pretty tricky. You know how to get close to the enemy without being seen and can steal his horses before he knows you're there."

Bouyer signed the same message to the Crows. The Rees appeared delighted at the words of praise. The Crows were not immune to the flattery, either—though one of the older ones, Iss-too-sah-shee-dah (Half Yellow Face), muttered darkly.

Custer cocked an inquiring eyebrow toward Mitch Bouyer.

"He says 'too many,' " the husky guide translated.

Custer nodded and turned away.

"To the best of my knowledge, the Indian camp lies to the west over that divide," Custer told his assembled company commanders, pointing to the gap in the Wolf Mountains a little further south and west of their temporary camp. "They're probably camped in the valley of the Little Big Horn about thirty miles or less from here. Where in that valley, I can't say with certainty. The trail ahead is fresh—indicating that we are very close."

The balding, former Civil War cavalry general looked at each of his twelve commanders in turn.

"From this point on, we are in the territory of the hostile scouts. It is imperative that we not be discovered until we are in a position to make a move against the camp. After dark, we will be fairly safe from discovery, but during the daylight hours, we must take precautions against a premature stampeding of the hostile camp."

The twelve men looked impatient in the sweltering summer sun and waved distractedly at swarms of insects that tormented them as Custer explained his reasons for abandoning the scout and his intentions to strike the enemy camp at the first opportunity. They rose without a murmur and almost listlessly attended to their own commands. But there was an almost surreptitious tightening of belts and they spat more in the space of ten minutes than they had in the previous two days.

The column led out—moving a trifle faster.

At five in the afternoon, they crossed to the right bank of the Rosebud and saw for themselves the heavy, fresh trail the scouts had reported. The valley narrowed and the trail widened until it took up the entire valley with pony tracks, droppings, and lodgepole trailings. The ground resembled a plowed field and even the newest recruits scanned the ominous horizon anxiously.

The horses walked at a rapid gait for almost three hours, heading nearly due west. At 7:45 the 7th Cavalry halted for camp. The scouts ranged ahead to ensure that the trail crossed the divide without splitting or turning off in a different direction.

"Come here, old man," Myles Keough told red-eyed Captain Fred Benteen jocularly as the latter straggled in. "I've kept the nicest spot in the whole camp next to me for your troop and I've had to bluff the balance to hold it. But here it is . . ." He gestured to a small draw surrounded on three sides by bluffs and close to the river. It looked green and inviting.

Benteen looked surprised and searched the Irishman's face for the rest of the joke. Keough mock-saluted.

"Skip off," he said lightly, "it's yours."

But the exchange was all that was light that evening. It was a silent, somber camp. The horseplay of the first evening was gone and a minimum of words were exchanged between the men as they mechanically went through the motions of setting up a tactical bivouac.

Swarthy Dan Newell, a private in M Company, was swimming in the Rosebud and came out of the water into the chilly atmosphere of the camp. His friend, Henry Scollin, was writing in a diary.

Newell laughed at the gloomy expression on his friend's face.

"What in the hell are you thinking about?" he asked as he replaced his underclothes. "You don't count on dying, do you?"

Scollin looked up from his diary with a stricken look.

"Dan," he said quietly, "if anything happens to me, notify my sister Mary, who lives in Gardiner, Massachusetts. My real name is Henry Cody. Scollin is assumed."

Newell didn't ask why. He merely nodded solemnly at the unexpected confidential disclosure.

Tall, stately Lieutenant William Cooke joined Frank Gibson, the practical joker, who was chatting animatedly with dark young Second Lieutenant James Garland Sturgis. "Jack" Sturgis was the son of the nominal commander of the 7th Cavalry. He had graduated from West Point only the year before, a small, baby-faced youngster of twenty-two. Gibson and Sturgis stopped their raillery and reminiscing as Cooke solemnly handed a piece of paper to Gibson.

"Gib," the Canadian with the enormous side whiskers whispered, "this is my will and I want you to witness it."

"What?" Gibson replied, laughing. "Getting cold feet, Cookey? After all these years with the savages?"

Cooke didn't smile.

"No," he said somberly, "but I have a feeling that the next fight will be my last."

"Oh, listen to the old woman," young Jack Sturgis commented. "Bet he's been to see a fortune teller."

Gibson looked into the eyes of the adjutant and his intended quip died on his lips. He nodded slowly.

A little while later, Sturgis' company commander, stocky "Fresh" Smith, joined the two. Cooke had gone. Sturgis laughingly related the incident. Smith removed a watch with a fob featuring a gold horse.

"Gib," he recited the ritual joke lightly, "if I am killed first, I will this fob to you. And if you go first, I get your bloodstone ring."

"And if you're both killed," young Sturgis inquired, "then who gets the loot?"

The older men laughed a little hollow. They didn't answer.

Private John McGuire of Tom Custer's C Company was settling in close to the scout camp. He looked up to find Mitch Bouyer, the half-breed guide, staring at him.

"We really close?" McGuire wanted to know.

Bouyer nodded.

"Be glad to get it over and done with?"

"There are too many for this outfit," Bouyer said flatly. "If we ever get up to them, they will recognize me and it will be the last of old Bouyer." He sighed raggedly. "Nevertheless, I have been drawing ten dollars per day from the government and I intend to stick it out."

The distinctive battle flag outside Custer's tent kept falling down, despite the fact that there was little or no wind. Big-nosed Ed Godfrey of K Company picked it up and planted it.

It fell again.

Godfrey picked it up and screwed it into the ground. It was starkly simple—a five-foot-by-three-foot swallowtail banner: red over blue, made of silk and featuring a pair of crossed sabers in white. It was George Armstrong Custer's personal battle flag—a prerogative of his as a brevet major general. Sergeant Hughes, a middle-aged Irishman in Godfrey's company, customarily carried it.

Godfrey stared uneasily at it as he backed away. It didn't fall again.

Captain Benteen settled down comfortably minus his boots and listened with half an ear as DeRudio and Keough reminisced about the Italian war for the second night in a row. He yawned.

"Two nights in a row without sleep," he explained to his bemused companions. "And I have a feeling GAC is cooking up a night march for us. He did it at the Washita and he'd do it again. Hate to be rude, but I'm an old man who needs his beauty rest." He rolled himself up in a blanket without another word, ignoring the snide remarks of the two soldiers of fortune.

His eyes had just closed when he heard an orderly calling in the dusk for Lieutenant Godfrey.

"He's right over by that tree," a trooper said.

The orderly blundered over to where Benteen lay.

"Lieutenant Godfrey?"

Benteen sat up—like a rudely wakened bear.

"Do I look like Godfrey?" he growled. "What is it?"

"I was told to find Lieutenant Godfrey and inform him that there is an officers' call at General Custer's right away, sir."

The orderly was a young man, trying valiantly to grow a mustache. Benteen sighed.

"Okay, son," he said softly, "I'll tell your lieutenant if I see him. He was over that direction earlier." He pointed toward a clump of trees closer to the river. The orderly saluted, stammered an apology for waking the senior captain of the regiment, and scurried off in the gathering darkness.

When the young man was safely out of earshot, Benteen exploded sulphurously. Keough and DeRudio hastened to him.

"I told you," he told them mock-angrily, "no rest for the wicked. Officers' call. Want to bet it is a night march?"

The Italian and Irishman declined to place bets. The three hurried off in search of Custer's tent.

When Benteen and the others arrived, Custer was already gone.

"It's a night march," Win Edgerly told them.

Reno bustled up.

"Are you commands ready?" he demanded.

"We're always ready, Major," Benteen replied lightly.

"You're not," Edgerly told Keough with a steady smile. "You've got the packtrain escort."

Keough cursed fluently. Benteen laughed.

"Skip off," he told the slender, dark-haired Irishman mockingly. "I can hear them braying from here. They need mother's love."

Somehow, in the haste and confusion, the six hundred and some soldiers, dozen or so civilians, and nearly fifty Indian scouts got on the trail in the pitch-black summer night. There was no moon and precious little coordination. They moved forward rapidly, so rapidly that the trailing companies were forced to trot. The lead and trail men of each company banged cups or pans on their saddle cantles to give the companies before and behind something to guide on in the dark.

In the blackness, many men—at times, whole companies—wandered off the trail and into thick underbrush. Loud profanity vied with the irritated snorting of abused horses for counterpoint to the chorus of braying mules in the rear.

They halted abruptly with no word of explanation from the head of the column. The water was so alkaline that the horses and mules wouldn't drink and their violent rejection caused a chorus of anger and frustration that Custer and his command party could hear two miles ahead. Custer trotted back to A Company and sought out Captain Myles Moylan.

"Send DeRudio and an orderly back down the trail to Captain Keough. Tell him to close up the packs."

Minutes later, DeRudio and Trumpeter William Hardy of A Company were running their horses as fast as they dared in the total darkness toward the packtrain. They found Keough with little difficulty, guiding on his rich Irish brogue raised in anger.

Keough was lamenting to a grinning, unsympathetic Benteen.

"General Custer wants you to move the packs as fast as you can," DeRudio informed the thoroughly exasperated Keough.

Benteen forestalled the coming explosion with a cheery remark: "Well, just do the best you can. I had them the first day out and it was no picnic. Dismount some of your troopers," he suggested, "and have them pull the jackasses across."

Keough let out a ragged breath.

"That's the most intelligent sound I've heard tonight, old man."

Benteen grinned, patted the Irishman on the back, and trotted forward.

On the return trip, DeRudio kept halting.

"It's this way, sir," Trumpeter Hardy said impatiently after the third such stop. Hardy was a fair-haired young man in his mid-twenties with a long blond mustache.

"I know where eet ees," DeRudio replied briefly.

"Then why are we halting?"

"You haf a white horse. I am afraid we weel be meestaken for Eendians."

The two rode on, stopping frequently.

Suddenly, off to one side of the trail, four "Eendians" surrounded the two messengers. They whooped in a subdued manner and began talking excitedly in a tongue DeRudio recognized as neither English nor Italian. He drew his pistol and cocked it.

A high-pitched laugh followed the sudden still silence that the pistol produced.

"Who goes there?" Captain Tom Custer demanded.

"Tom? Tom?" DeRudio asked. "Ees that you?"

"None other," the general's brother answered. "The Rees here thought you were hostile scouts." He laughed again—the merriment of relieved tension. "What are you doing here? Are you lost?"

Trumpeter Hardy began to laugh—loudly.

DeRudio tried to glare at him in the dark, but it had no effect.

"We are carrying messages for the general," DeRudio replied stiffly.

"Well, you gave me a scare," Tom Custer chuckled.

"You gave us a beeger scare," DeRudio insisted, joining the relieved laughter.

The 7th Cavalry halted a second time alongside a small stream. The troubled horses and mules were allowed to drink. The exhausted troopers lay down, wrapping the reins around their left arms, and tried to catch the stolen sleep.

No orders came down from the head of the column, so the packs and saddles remained on. Some of the companies closest to the head of the column built fires and the others followed suit. The mules wandered and poorly tied packs slid. Some fell off. The harried packers couldn't keep up with it and after a while gave up completely.

Morning—
Sunday, June 25, 1876

Second Lieutenant Charles A. Varnum and his eleven-man scout detail reached the Crow's Nest about 2:30 A.M. There was no moonlight, but a little more illumination from the stars was an aid to vision once they climbed out of the narrow valley and ascended the west slope of the geological freak that the Indians had used as an observation post for generations. One side of the steep hill was bare—and here the horses were picketed. The men left the horses in the care of two Ree youngsters, Black Fox and Bull, and climbed the peak. Mitch Bouyer and a big-bellied Crow of middle age named White Swan led the way.

Varnum rubbed his red-rimmed small black eyes and lay down to catch some sleep until the sun in the east peeped up enough to allow them to see the ground to the west. He was vaguely aware of the grumbling Crows pointing out the roaring fires of the Custer column—visible plainly to the north and east. Besides White Swan, there were two other Crows—an experienced scout named White Man Runs Him and a youth named Shes-his, or Curley. Lonesome Charlie Reynolds, his arm still in a sling, supervised the remaining Rees: Bear, Strike Bear, and Strike the Lodge. Their nominal leader was thirty-seven-year-old Arri-chitt, or Forked Horn. They made little noise and the younger ones studied the black night, while the old campaigners followed Varnum's example and tried to catch a few winks.

Bouyer woke Varnum in a couple of hours. The eerie false light of the pre-dawn and the clear skies common to eastern Montana enabled them to see many miles to the west. For about fifteen miles, the ground resembled a washboard from their high vantage point—with narrow gulches and coulees flanked by impossibly steep ridges and hills. A belt of darker-colored flatland could be seen somewhere between fifteen and twenty miles west.

"Little Big Horn," Bouyer informed the scout commander. "See the camp?"

Varnum strained his sore eyes mightily. He shook his head.

"See the smoke from their fires?" Bouyer persisted.

"I see them," Charlie Reynolds said. Varnum agreed that the mist he saw in the direction indicated was Sioux campfire smoke.

The Crows and Rees were talking excitedly. Varnum, who understood some of their language, recognized the phrase "pony herd."

"Where is it?" he demanded.

"Look for worms," Bouyer advised him. "They look like thousands of brown worms from here."

Varnum couldn't see, but began to scribble a note to Custer.

The two Rees dispatched were Strike Bear, a twenty-one-year-old, and the youth, Bull, who had guarded the scouts' horses. Strike Bear rode a cavalry mount and Bull lagged behind on a small Indian pony. Strike Bear went straight to the advance camp of the scouts who had remained with the column, arriving after the sun had been up for almost three hours. The other scouts were brewing breakfast—mostly coffee—and Strike Bear found himself the enviable center of attention as he calmly helped himself to a mug of skalljaw and gave grunting, monosyllabic replies to the curious questions.

Fred F. Gerard, the forty-six-year-old post interpreter from Fort Lincoln, had not been able to sleep well and he awoke with an irritated scowl as the boot prodded his moccasins none too gently. The man wearing the boot was Lieutenant Colonel George Armstrong Custer. Custer's face was flushed with excitement.

"Gerard, get up," he said. "Some of the scouts have come in from the high point and I think we should get up there."

"There" turned out to be the forward camp of the scouts, where Strike Bear was having his story confirmed by the youthful Bull, who had just come in. The Indians began to strip and redress themselves in their "war" shirts. Out came the medicine

bags sacred to each individual and a murmur of solemn anticipation accompanied the ritual.

Custer strode into the camp with his customary briskness. He
was smiling and in an apparently good mood. He was flanked by
Gerard and scar-faced Tom Custer. After an exchange of pleas-
antries, Custer sought out expressionless Bloody Knife. With a
broad smile and a wink at Tom Custer, he directed Bloody
Knife's attention toward the younger brother.

"Your brother is frightened," he told his favorite Indian scout,
meaning his own brother, Tom. "His heart flutters with fear. His
eyes are rolling with fright at this news of the Sioux."

The Indians listening were much amused. Tom Custer grinned
good-naturedly, used to the teasing of his famous older brother.
Even dour Bloody Knife smiled slightly.

"When we have beaten the Sioux," Custer went on, "he will
then be a man."

Bloody Knife responded gutturally in Ree without hesitation.

"What's that he says?" Custer inquired of Gerard.

"He says we'll find enough Sioux to keep us fighting two or
three days."

Custer smiled.

"Oh, I guess we'll get through with them in one day," he said
lightly.

He took Varnum's note from Strike Bear almost casually, having observed the protocol—the appearing disinterested as he joked
with Bloody Knife. The nostrils of his fleshy nose flared, but he
gave no other outward indication of his reaction to the note.

At that moment, Sergeant Major William Sharrow, a thirty-
year-old blond who uncannily resembled Tom Custer and was the
senior noncommissioned officer in the regiment, appeared with
the orderlies for the day. These were the young men selected from
the companies for their outstanding personal appearance and attention to equipment. Two trumpeters—Dose from G Company
and Martin from Benteen's H Company—were the honored ones.
Custer nodded distractedly.

Within minutes, accompanied by Fred Gerard and two Rees,
Custer mounted to follow the messenger, Strike Bear, back to the
Crow's Nest. The Rees selected for Custer's escort were Bob-
Tailed Bull, wearing his blue blouse with sergeant's stripes

proudly, and a tough-looking younger man named Little Brave. Bob-Tailed Bull was forty-five, past fighting age for an Indian, but his experience and standing with the younger men made him a natural leader—though a somewhat comical-appearing one.

The command party started out. The adjutant, Cooke, called out anxiously, "Is the command to follow?"

"No," Custer told him sharply, "you will remain here until I return."

Near the rear of the column, Reno and his erstwhile adjutant, Benny Hodgson, were brewing coffee and toasting hardtack. Captain Benteen, who had had no luck as an early-morning fisherman, invited himself to help wolf down breakfast. The mules were restive and representatives from the twelve companies were rounding up the ones carrying food—to fix breakfast for the hungry troopers further along the line. Except for the swearing and hee-hawing in the distance, Benteen and his hosts enjoyed a quiet breakfast together.

"I wonder when GAC is going to reinstitute the battalion formations?" Reno asked.

Benteen shrugged. "Probably tomorrow when he completes his surround of the Indians and is ready to attack. You'll get the easy charge. I'll spend another night wandering through the dark looking for a place to cross some damned stream. I'll get the far side of the surround—the long way around." He laughed sourly.

"Like at the Washita?" Hodgson chuckled.

Benteen's eyes didn't smile with his lips. "Like at the Washita," he agreed.

Captain Yates, the burly blond commander of F Company, wandered up.

"Major, the general has gone up to the lookout. A few of our packs are missing and one of my sergeants wants to go back along our trail and see if he can find them." He eyed Reno uncertainly. "If that is okay with you, sir."

Reno rolled his hand in the universal "go on" gesture. Yates walked stiffly away. Reno turned to Hodgson.

"I am afraid that General Custer has left us here to our own devices while he is off on a scout of some kind. Now, with the enemy close at hand as all signs indicate, should we not mount the command and ready them for a hard chase?"

Reno was speaking to Hodgson, but it was Benteen who answered after young Benny merely nodded and rolled his eyes around to get the opinion of the senior captain. Reno himself was looking at Benteen out of the corner of his eye as he put his comment and question to Hodgson.

"If I were you, I would do nothing," Benteen said, "until Mr. Lo is found. Tracks in the sand are one thing. I've followed them for almost ten campaigns now. They don't always lead to a scrape with Indians. We could be following this one all summer and all the way to the Pacific Ocean and never see an actual Indian. No," he continued, shaking his large, snowy-maned head, "I wouldn't start chasing until GAC gives the word."

Reno jerked his head impatiently.

Benteen smiled knowingly at young Hodgson, who was studying the clear bright skies with glazed eyes.

"Glad to be away from it?" he asked.

Hodgson studied the older man's smiling face with an embarrassed and outraged look that vanished in the face of Benteen's level-eyed stare. Benteen's smile never flickered. Hodgson blew out his breath raggedly.

"When I left Louisiana," he declared quietly, "I felt the weight of a mountain had been lifted from my shoulders." He stood and walked away from the two older men without another glance in their direction.

"What was that all about?" Reno demanded sharply.

Benteen kept smiling. "Oh, young Benny went a-chasin' the musky fox and she turned on him. It's a good thing the campaign came along when it did. He wouldn't have lasted much longer."

Reno was all curiosity.

"You mean Emiline Bell?" he asked. "I knew Benny got his head turned over some woman. He even tendered his resignation to get out. What do you know about it?"

"More than a gentleman should," Benteen answered drily.

"Who is this 'musky fox'? Mrs. Bell?"

Benteen shook his large white head reprovingly, still smiling.

"Ask Wallace about it," he suggested.

Reno appeared to lose interest in the conversation.

"I still think we should be moving," he murmured aloud.

Sergeant William A. Curtiss of F Company was a dark brown man in his early thirties. He wore a swooping mustache of the style referred to as "dragoon's." The rest of his face was unshaven and dark stubble covered his leathery-skinned chin. He was looking for a lost food pack. There were two men with him, both Irish immigrants older than himself. They walked their horses at a moderate rate back over the trail taken by the column during the night.

As they swung around the base of a small hill covered with sagebrush, they spotted the lost pack. An Indian was squatting beside the box that had fallen by the wayside and was prying the lid off with a hatchet.

Curtiss whooped and galloped toward him. Suddenly, two other Indians sprang up from the tall grass beside the trail. Curtiss fired one shot with his carbine and then emptied his pistol. The two Irishmen trotted after him, numb with surprise. One of the Indians staggered and slipped. Curtiss abandoned the chase and returned to the pack in the middle of the trail.

It was a box of hardtack. A single nibbled piece lay in the churned-up sand of the trail. Curtiss dismounted and scooped up the box. He handed it to one of the Irish troopers. He looked at the hill the Indians were last seen climbing to get away from his hot, but erratic, fire. He kicked the discarded piece of hardtack.

"Dammit," he said to no one in particular, "they found us."

At almost the same time, Varnum's scouts in the Crow's Nest spotted three other Indians. One was apparently alone. The other two seemed to be looking for stray ponies, as both were mounted and one was leading a third horse with a rope halter. The Crows and Rees began to talk at once.

"They'll spot the column," Bouyer said to Varnum.

Varnum's black eyes gleamed. "They're headed this way. Can't we ambush them?"

Reynolds chipped in. "If they haven't spotted anything and we miss, they are sure to report us."

"Well, don't miss," Varnum snapped.

The scouts were already clambering down the steep hill and jogging in the direction of the hostiles. Some went around behind to mount their ponies and lead the others to the impatient ones. Varnum was afoot.

Reynolds watched the maneuver from atop the lookout, shaking his head.

The Indians had disappeared over a hill in the direction of the Little Big Horn by the time Custer appeared in the draw at the base of the Crow's Nest. Varnum, still afoot, greeted him.

"They didn't see anything?" Custer asked sharply when Varnum reported the episode. "Are you sure?"

Varnum replied positively and not a little vehemently.

Custer grinned. "Well, you have had a night of it," he said as the two climbed to the top of the lookout.

Varnum rubbed his sore eyes.

"Yes," he replied, "but I am still able to sit up and notice things."

Custer clapped him affectionately on the shoulder.

Custer couldn't see anything and he appealed to a glum Charlie Reynolds.

"My eyes are not that good any more," Reynolds answered morosely.

Gerard handed Custer a cheap telescope borrowed from one of the scouts. After a while, Custer handed it back.

"I don't see anything," he concluded.

The column moved out—toward the divide. Cooke protested Reno's order to march formally and then maintained a stiff-lipped silence as he rode beside Tom Custer. Few words were exchanged.

Myles Keough rode up between them so suddenly they were startled. Tom Custer instinctively reached for his pistol and then relaxed as he recognized Keough, white-lipped and unsmiling for a change.

"One of Yates's noncoms ran into a party of Sioux rifling one of the packs about five miles back," he said grimly.

Tom Custer swore softly.

Cooke spoke. "The general should be informed at once."

"I say again we have not been seen," Custer said heatedly to White Swan through Mitch Bouyer. The group atop the Crow's Nest were seated on the lip of a ledge, staring intently west toward the valley of the Little Big Horn.

"The camp has not seen us," he repeated, a little more subdued. "I want to wait until dark and then we will march. We will place our army around the Sioux camp." He described the tactic with his hands.

White Swan spoke and Bouyer translated.

"That plan is bad," the veteran scout told Custer, "it should not be carried out."

"I have said what I plan to do," Custer snapped.

There was a chilly silence. In the background, Charlie Reynolds rummaged through his saddlebag, fingering his personal belongings with a faraway look in his eyes.

"Well," Custer sighed, "I've got as good eyes as anyone and I can't see any village, Indians, or anything."

"Well, General," Bouyer said evenly, "if you don't find more Indians in that valley than you ever saw, you can hang me!"

Custer flushed and sprang to his feet, lifting a weary Varnum up without seeing him. "It would do a damn sight of good to hang you, wouldn't it?" he said sarcastically to the half-breed.

Bouyer stiffened and Varnum whitened. Custer strode off and headed down the reverse slope. Varnum stopped at Charlie Reynolds' feet.

"That's odd," he mused aloud. "I've only heard Custer use the word 'damn' once before in my life. He's really upset, I can tell. What are you doing?"

Reynolds was passing out items from his saddlebags to the Indians.

"I won't be needing these after today," the quiet man said grimly.

As they walked down from the lookout to their horses below, Mitch Bouyer fell in beside Custer.

"General," he said quietly, almost apologetically, "I have been with these Indians for thirty years and this is the largest village I have ever known. Too large for your command."

Custer waved impatiently. "You're not a soldier. You need not go in," he said airily.

Bouyer's already dark face purpled. "General," he said thickly, "I am not afraid to go in with you anywhere, but if we go into that valley, we will both wake up in hell!"

"All right—all right—all right—all right," Custer stammered absently.

It was nearly eleven in the morning by the time Custer came in sight of the command. Cooke and Tom Custer were trotting toward him.

Custer murmured to Gerard, "Now, who in mischief moved that command?"

Varnum, a few yards behind, overheard the exchange and moved forward when he heard the angry Custer moderate his language as he usually did. He winked at Charlie Reynolds when he passed him as if to say, "It's all right now."

"Tom," Custer called to his brother when they were within earshot, "who moved the command?"

Tom Custer glanced sidelong at Cooke and, seeing no support forthcoming, said stiffly, "I don't know. The orders were to march and we marched."

Before Custer could reply to this, Cooke spoke up.

"General, we've been spotted by hostile scouts."

Custer didn't explode. He seemed to pale and looked strangely wan.

"Yates told Keough and we thought you'd want to know right away," Tom Custer concluded.

Major Reno hove into view. Cooke and Tom Custer exchanged uneasy glances, but Custer seemed not to see the dark-faced major.

Keough came up and explained the experience of Sergeant Curtiss. Custer turned in his saddle and sought out Varnum.

"Could they have been the ones you saw?" he demanded.

Varnum took a deep breath and shook his head. "The ones were watching never got near the column, let alone behind it. And they didn't seem to be in any hurry. I know Curtiss. He's a good shot. Even mounted, he would have pinked one of them. The ones we saw hadn't been shot at, I'm sure."

Custer nodded. "I'm sure you're right," he said mildly, and dismounted. He gestured at Cooke, who was preparing to dismount also.

"No," he said, "I want the officers here—right here . . . right now. All of them."

Cooke galloped off.

Private Charles Windolph, a stocky, sandy-haired German immigrant in H Company, moved toward the knot of officers around Custer. Windolph was looking for Captain Benteen, his own company commander, with a request to be permitted to exchange horses with another man. He stopped cold when he heard Benteen's voice off to one side.

"Hadn't we better keep the regiment together, General?" Benteen was saying to Custer. "If this is as big a camp as they say, we'll need every man we have."

"You have your orders," Custer said.

Windolph faded back out of earshot.

The officers continued to straggle into the council of war. Custer was in the middle of describing his view from the Crow's Nest when DeRudio came up. Cooke pulled the little Italian aside.

"Do you still have those Austrian glasses?" the adjutant asked, and as DeRudio nodded dazedly, he added in a whisper, "The general wants them." Reluctantly, DeRudio gave them to Cooke for Custer.

"I want to be sure that every man in every company is armed in accordance with my instructions at the Yellowstone when we started out," Custer said in his rapid, high-pitched voice. "I want company commanders to personally see to it that my orders have been complied with by all.

"Lastly," he concluded, "I want no more than one noncom and six enlisted men per company in the packtrains. The first officer to report his company in compliance with my instructions will have the advance. The last will have to escort the packs."

He waved his hands in dismissal.

The officers moved away rapidly—some of them scurrying. Gus Mathey encountered the first group and listened to hasty explanations as he hurried after them with questions. Potbellied Tom Weir of D Company and lean Ed Godfrey of K Company were practically in a footrace.

One officer didn't move from the gathering. He stood, staring coolly at Custer, with a grin on his face. Captain Fred Benteen of H Company saluted casually.

"What is it?" Custer snapped impatiently.

"Well, General," Benteen drawled, his smile not altering, "it seems that H is ready."

Custer glared at the insouciant senior captain and opened his mouth. He closed it again with a snap and, unable to hold the challenging stare of the older man, dropped his eyes.

"Well, Colonel Benteen," he said firmly, after an awkward pause, "your troop has the advance."

Custer mounted his horse in one fluid motion and started back down the column aimlessly. He looked at the still-smiling Benteen as he went past. And nodded.

George Herendeen awoke from a catnap to the sight and sound of something scurrying up the face of the hill opposite the little draw where he had been lying.

"See that Indian?" Mitch Bouyer called.

"Indian?" Herendeen asked, looking around with alarm. "Are you sure it wasn't a deer?"

"It was an Indian," Bouyer informed him, "and when he saw you, he run for camp."

Herendeen cinched his horse and mounted carefully as if in a trance. He followed the stocky half-breed forward, staring intently at the line of ridges to all sides.

Captain Tom McDougall was the last company commander to report and was assigned to the packtrain to escort Mathey and his much-reinforced packers. One sergeant and six men from each of the companies joined the packs. H Company's contingent was led in personally by Lieutenant Frank Gibson. They were among the last to report. This caused some grumbling on the part of other commanders who had bothered to check out their commands in accordance with Custer's instructions and who had delayed reporting until their details had reported for duty. They received position assignments well to the rear.

"I just obey orders," Gibson told Lieutenant Jim Calhoun as he rode past L Company on his way back to the head of the column where Captain Benteen waited. Incredibly, Tom Weir had won the footrace with Godfrey and was assigned second place in the column.

"You left no instructions," Reno protested to an angry Custer.

"You are in error," Custer stammered. "The last thing I said before I left was that the command was to remain where it was. If your insubordination is the cause of the hostiles escaping, I promise you there will be charges."

Reno's eyes snapped, but he pressed his mouth closed in a thin line and said nothing.

Custer stared at him.

"As usual, you offer no explanation," he said.

"What's the use?" Reno answered with his eyes unfocused over Custer's shoulder and his lip curled.

Custer seemed on the verge of exploding and then, suddenly, his shoulders sagged perceptibly. Reno's eyes flickered momentarily as he took this in. Custer looked at his sullen second-in-command much the way he had looked at the insouciant Captain Benteen earlier—with narrow-eyed thoughtfulness.

"Your aggressiveness could prove useful before the day is over," Custer said quietly, speculatively.

Reno stared incredulously at his commanding officer's back as Custer rode forward toward the head of the column. Benny Hodgson sidled up. He looked at his erstwhile commander with an engaging grin.

"Will you be needing my services, Major? Or should I join the packs?"

Reno looked at the banty rooster with the bushy mustache fondly. "You had duty last night, Benny. And I have no command." Noting the crestfallen look on the younger man's face, he added quickly with a sardonic smile, "But I may have one yet. And when it comes, I won't refuse any volunteers."

He shook his young protégé by the hand, blinking.

Afternoon—
Sunday, June 25, 1876

Benteen led out at a walk on his long-legged blood bay, Dick. The horse walked abnormally fast and Benteen appeared not to notice as he scanned the ridges front and side for Indians. Behind him, the column moved forward rapidly. Custer was deep in conference with Cooke and the scouts were ranging far to the front.

They crossed the divide between the Rosebud Valley and the Little Big Horn Valley without much notice and certainly no ceremony. Second Lieutenant Nick Wallace, the itinerarist, noted that it was just after noon Chicago time. The troopers began jettisoning the two-gallon nose bags filled with oats that were tied to the necks of their mounts. Sergeants protested angrily, but it was continued surreptitiously anyway.

The pack mules under Lieutenant Mathey and the escort under Captain McDougall lagged. Benny Hodgson conferred for a moment with the roly-poly Captain Mac and then galloped up the column to join Major Reno, who, with straw hat pushed back on his forehead, was chivying troops enthusiastically. The sun was not yet directly overhead, as it was still not noon Montana time, but it was already hot. The heat of the Montana highlands was dry and not unbearable, but certainly uncomfortable. The troops began removing their tunics and rolling up the sleeves of their gray flannel undershirts. The ones who wore the 1872-issue black hats unpinned them and the flimsy, wide brims flopped with each step the horses took. They looked like a column of scarecrows, riding four abreast. Now and then a blue tunic or buckskin could be seen or a white wool or straw hat, but in the main the 7th Cavalry looked like a formation of saddle bums. And they might have been for all that, except that saddle bums were not known to struggle to keep in formation or to keep up with the lead element.

Benteen hadn't gone too far when Custer appeared beside him. "Colonel," Custer said with an embarrassed grin, "you're setting too fast a pace."

Benteen slowed his fast-walking horse and the two men rode side by side for some distance in silence. Custer was on the verge of saying something on two occasions, and Benteen, watching out of the corner of his eye, noticed the hesitation.

Abruptly, Custer turned back without a word and began to talk earnestly with Lieutenant Cooke. Cooke trotted away from Custer after the brief conference. He encountered Reno halfway down the column taking an active part in pushing the lagging men and horses.

"The general directs you to take specific command of Companies A, G, and M," the long-whiskered Canadian told the tall, pudgy major.

"Is that all?" Reno asked sharply.

"That is all," Cooke intoned, and trotted off without a backward glance.

Lieutenant Hare and Fred Gerard worked the right-hand side of the column with most of the Rees. Lieutenant Varnum still stayed on the left-hand side of the trail. Varnum was accompanied by Mitch Bouyer and the Crows.

They ranged far in front of the column of fours that was the 7th Cavalry.

Lieutenant Cooke sent a red-brassarded orderly back down the column to the packs with instructions to keep the mules off the trail as much as possible as they were raising so much dust. As he made his way back up toward the head of the column, he passed this advice to every company commander he encountered. As a result, the men were echeloned to either side of the well-defined trail as much as possible. Not only did it cut down on the amount of dust they raised to be seen for miles, but it also cut down on the amount of dust they had to eat. They were spared much of the dust kicked up by the hooves of the horses in the preceding companies.

Still, there was a lot of dust, and within minutes the gray-shirted troopers looked brownish red, covered as they were with trail dust. Many continued to affect the bandanna-over-the-mouth-and-nose style of the road agent. They walked at varying speeds. The fast pace initially set by Benteen caused them to accordion badly. After he had slowed down in accordance with Custer's orders, the troopers and their mounts began to bunch.

Cooke called Benteen aside and pointed to a long ridgeline running almost perpendicular to the line of march, but a long distance to the south and west.

"Proceed to that line of bluffs," he told the white-haired Benteen. "Pitch into anything you come across. Send word back to General Custer if you come across anything."

Benteen obliqued to the left with his own H Company and Companies D (Weir) and K (Godfrey). He looked balefully at the lithe buckskin figure that was Custer, once again assuming the lead of the column. He didn't see Major Reno appear beside him.

"Where are you going, Benteen?" Reno asked.

Benteen waved a hand airily in the general direction his three-company battalion was headed.

"I'm to pitch into anything I find."

"What if you don't find anything?"

Benteen laughed knowingly. "In that case, I'll be well out of the way if the circus begins."

Reno rode beside him for a little way. "I think the general is probing to his left as he was ordered to by General Terry," Reno said at last.

Benteen snorted. "I'm not looking for any trails," he said heavily. "I'm looking for live Indians. What are you doing?"

"I have taken command of Companies A, G, and M."

Benteen stared at him. "Is that all?"

"That was my question," Reno answered, "and I was told, quote: 'That is all.'"

Benteen lifted his eyebrows fractionally as he cantered forward to direct Lieutenant Frank Gibson to mount the high ground ahead with a six-man vedette. Reno turned back to supervise his own command.

Marcus Kellogg, the middle-aged reporter, was riding a mule rapidly to the front. Fred Gerard, the black-eyed interpreter, hailed him.

"Fred," the newshound asked seriously, "could I borrow those spurs you've got in your pack? I want to keep up with the scouts."

Gerard handed him the spurs.

"Shouldn't you stay with the command? It could be dangerous up here. You should have an adequate escort."

Kellogg laughed. "Where's your escort?"

"We don't need one," Gerard replied evenly. "If the hostiles appear in force, we run. Our job is to find them and maybe run off a few ponies. We're not supposed to fight them. You won't be able to run very fast on that mule. Besides, all the action will be back with the column and Custer."

"I'm expecting some interesting developments," Kellogg replied seriously, "and I want to keep up with the scouts."

He attached the borrowed spurs to his boots and put them to use, leaving Gerard behind.

George Herendeen, the young cowboy attached to the command by General Terry, reined in beside Custer. The commander was scanning the ridges to the front and paid him scant attention.

"General," Herendeen said apologetically at last, "the head of Tulloch's Creek is just over yonder."

Custer looked at him annoyedly, but spoke in a patient tone.

"Yes, but there are no Indians in that direction. They are all in our front. And besides, they have discovered us."

Herendeen was about to interrupt, but Custer's high-pitched, stammering voice went on incisively.

"It will be of no use to send you down Tulloch's Creek. The only thing to do is to push ahead and attack the camp as soon as possible."

Cooke rode all the way back to the packtrain and accosted Lieutenant Mathey.

"Did you get the order to stay off the trail?" he asked.

"Yes," Mathey answered, pointing out the arrangement of the mules. They were off the trail—more or less. "How's that?"

"That's better," Cooke replied uncertainly. "They're not kicking up so much dust."

He galloped forward.

Lieutenant Gibson rode in front of Benteen's three-company column with six men. They investigated the ridgetops as hurriedly as they could, but due to the roughness of the terrain, they had difficulty keeping very far ahead. The battalion was forced to halt frequently to give them time to complete their mission and move on.

During the first such halt, the chief trumpeter, Sergeant Voss, galloped up to Benteen with Custer's compliments.

"If nothing is found upon reaching the first line of bluffs, proceed to the second line of bluffs with the same instructions," he recited.

"And then?" Benteen demanded.

"That's all I was told, sir," replied the blue-eyed, blond German immigrant.

Benteen cursed as he watched Voss gallop back toward the trail. He signaled Gibson and the three-company flank scout pushed on.

A mile later, Sergeant Major William Sharrow galloped up to Benteen with yet another message from Custer.

"If nothing is found at the second line of bluffs," Sharrow recited, "then proceed to the valley. And if there is nothing in that valley, go on to the next."

"Goddammit—" Benteen exploded, but Sergeant Major Sharrow cut him short with a crisp, cool reply.

"Those are the instructions I was given, sir."

Benteen sighed. "Carry on, Sergeant Major," he said coolly.

Sharrow, who was also blue-eyed and blond-haired like Voss before him and their commanding officer, galloped away.

"Junior Custer," Benteen growled to big Lieutenant Win Edgerly, who had ridden forward, his eyebrows raised in question. Captain Weir, who customarily gave Edgerly the commanding officer's position in the column, also hurried forward.

"What is it, Fred?" he asked quietly.

"It seems we are to go valley hunting ad infinitum," Benteen groused to the two officers of D Company. "We could go all the way to Fort Benton at this rate. Maybe that's where GAC wants me—punishment for speaking up. GAC has not sense enough to know that nothing is too hard for me that takes me away from his immediate proximity."

"That's not the general's way of doing things," Weir reproved the older man mildly.

"Well, we have our orders, senseless though they be," Benteen said with a sigh. Weir opened his mouth to protest, but Benteen spoke first. "There is no trail here and I can't for the life of me see Indians traveling over country this rough unless they had to go this way. The signs are that they didn't come this way at all. We'll go on to this second valley. Then I think we ought to look to going back to the main trail. Indians have too much sense for this kind of marching."

The two officers of D Company looked askance and Benteen swung his long-legged bay around savagely and led the battalion on.

The main column marched on, picking up speed with each half mile. It wasn't a conscious effort. The horses had their proverbial second wind and the troopers didn't restrain them.

Custer and Cooke were studying the terrain to the left as the column halted near a low spot partially filled with water holes. The horses lunged for the morass, but the cavalrymen, with an effort, kept them on the trail. Custer and Cooke rode at the front of the five companies on the right side of the little creek that ran generally east to west. Major Reno and Lieutenant Benny Hodgson rode at the head of three companies on the left-hand side of the creek.

"I wonder if Colonel Benteen will make it all the way to the valley through that," Cooke remarked to Custer as they studied the badlands to the south.

"Colonel Benteen is perhaps the best field commander in the regiment," Custer remarked matter-of-factly. "If he finds the going *too* rough, he will return to the trail."

"Sharrow reports that he was very exasperated."

Custer smiled. "Colonel Benteen has a very belligerent personality. His own father disowned him for joining the Union Army—"

Cooke groaned.

"If he told you that, General," he said, "that makes the regiment complete. He has told everyone else now. Several times."

"What he probably didn't tell you was that he was responsible for capturing his own father and his father's boats—depriving the older Benteen of a livelihood and condemning him to prison for the duration of the war."

Cooke raised his eyebrows. "No wonder he's so cantankerous. I always thought that it was a personal matter between him and, uh, well, other officers."

"Me?" Custer laughed. "No, we understand each other. He's a good soldier. As I said, the best. When he believes in something, he doesn't let sentiment stand in his way. He has a very strong sense of duty. I am aware that he dislikes me, but he doesn't let that interfere with his duty as he sees it."

Cooke was about to say something, when Custer gestured irritatedly.

"We haven't heard from the scouts. They must have something to report by now. Send the sergeant major up ahead with my compliments. I want a report."

Sergeant Major Sharrow found Lieutenant Luther Hare just as the latter discovered a Sioux burial lodge. The poles of a second lodge were still standing and the Rees crowded closer to look over the first one. They slit the buffalo hide and one of them entered the lone tepee, emerging with a buckskin trophy. The others gathered around and began talking volubly in their native tongue.

Hare looked up with surprise.

"General Custer's compliments," Sharrow addressed the rangy Texan. "He wonders why you haven't reported anything."

"There's nothing to report," Hare said.

Sharrow gestured at the lone tepee.

"Very well, Sergeant Major," Hare said evenly, "you can report that we have found a lodge with a good Indian inside it. It appears he was shot."

"It's too soon for General Terry to be up," Sharrow mused.

"They're probably running from Crook."

Sharrow pursed his lips and then wheeled his horse and galloped back down the trail.

Lieutenant Gibson joined Captain Benteen at the latter's signal just as Godfrey, Weir, and Edgerly trotted up.

"This is senseless," Benteen repeated. "If GAC finds the Indians he's trailing, he will need our services. There's nothing here but ridges and valleys. No Indians. We'd better join up with the others or we'll miss the fight—if there is to be one."

The other officers had nothing to say. They rejoined their companies as Benteen led off north toward the trail they had left earlier. They found the going difficult at first, but soon found themselves in column across the floor of a little valley and made good time—all except for Gibson and his six-man patrol on the ridgeline to the west.

Gerard was riding along a ridge to the north and west of the lone tepee when the five-company column under Custer arrived at the tepee. The Rees were gathered around, jabbering and painting themselves. Hare looked harassed.

"Why aren't the scouts forward where they belong?" Custer demanded of Hare.

Before Hare could reply, Gerard waved his hat and bellowed out, "There are your Indians, General! Running like the devil!"

The boisterous civilian wheeled his horse and galloped toward Custer.

"Lead out," Custer signed to Bloody Knife. The Rees saw the sign and began to talk excitedly among themselves. Varnum galloped back.

"The scouts should be an hour ahead of us," Custer complained to Varnum. "Move them out at once. Strike the camp! Drive off the horse herd! Why are they wasting time?"

Varnum shouted a few words in Ree. The scouts looked mutinous. Custer was livid.

"If they don't want to find the Sioux, dismount them. Send them back to the packs. Are they women?"

One of the scouts spoke up as Isaiah Dorman, the Negro, interpreted Custer's remarks.

"If Long Hair takes the horses of all his young braves who are not eager to die, he will have to fight the Sioux alone."

Gerard arrived as the rebellious remarks were being translated to an angry Custer.

"What's the matter?" he demanded.

Custer ignored him and, turning in his saddle, gestured at Major Reno on the other side of the creek. He waved his hat and beckoned Reno over. He moved away from the conference of stony-faced Rees in front of the lone tepee and spoke incisively to Cooke.

"We'll send Reno and his battalion in first."

He turned to Varnum.

"How far ahead is the valley?"

"A good couple of miles," Varnum replied, his pinched face even tighter than normal.

"Did you actually see the camp?"

"No, sir. But—"

"Locate it," Custer snapped. "Our guides have failed us. *Your* guides have failed us. Can't anyone follow orders in this regiment anymore?"

Varnum galloped off with alacrity.

Gerard, now on foot, walked over to Custer and looked up at him.

"There's been a misunderstanding, General," he said. "The Indians say we are almost at the village and they thought you meant for them to attack. They want the soldiers to come with them. They say the camp is too big for them alone."

Custer laughed without humor.

"Is that what they said, Gerard? Or are you putting words in their mouths?"

"General, they are saying they were hired to locate the camp and to drive off the ponies. They say they aren't supposed to fight the Sioux alone. They want to know why the soldiers aren't going with them."

"All right—all right—all right—all right," Custer murmured, and then, straightening in the saddle, began to speak incisively. "Tell them I am sending Major Reno on ahead to attack the village. Tell them I want them to be brave and show him the way— and maybe make off with some fine Sioux horses."

Custer was smiling and Gerard responded in kind as he pivoted and began to address the Rees in his harsh, loud voice.

Cooke intercepted Reno on the way to Custer.

"Gerard says the Indians are about two miles ahead and on the run," Cooke informed Reno. "The general directs you to take your three companies ahead as rapidly as you can. You are to charge the village. We will support you."

Reno waited for more and, as Cooke began to move back toward Custer, the dark-faced major called out plaintively.

"*Who* will support me?"

Cooke glanced back over his shoulder.

"The whole outfit," he replied matter-of-factly.

Reno flicked a glance at Custer, who was mingling with the now enthusiastic Indians. He turned and started back across the creek where Benny Hodgson and three company commanders were waiting for him. As he was about to call to his young adjutant, Reno heard Custer's high-pitched voice.

"Tell him to take the scouts."

He turned to see Charlie Reynolds hurrying toward him—with the Rees following in their customary individual ways.

"I know," he called to Reynolds before the guide could speak. "We are to take the scouts too."

Hodgson looked questioningly.

"We are to move forward as rapidly as we deem prudent and charge the village afterward. We will be supported by the whole outfit," Reno told him.

Hodgson flashed a grin and galloped toward the head of the three-company column, where Captains French and Moylan were waiting with Lieutenants McIntosh and DeRudio.

Back at the morass, Captain Weir was getting impatient. Benteen's three-company battalion had rejoined the trail there and were watering thirsty horses. A half hour after reaching the watering place, they were still there. Benteen looked up and down the trail and spotted the pack mules being escorted under Captain McDougall making their way slowly but surely to the morass. Weir noticed it too.

"I wonder what the old man is keeping us here so long for?" Weir asked his young giant second lieutenant, Winfield Edgerly.

The lead mules had run headlong into the swampy morass and promptly got stuck—braying happily in the water—while the soldiers and packers, cursing, tried to move the animals. Weir shook his head in disgust and looked around him in sudden decision.

"Move out," he told Lieutenant Edgerly, "we aren't waiting here any longer."

Benteen saw the move and hustled the other two companies after D Company. He caught up with Weir out of earshot of all but Edgerly.

"Tom," he asked with his smile never faltering, "are you going to win the fight all by yourself? Or would you like a little support?"

"The others were ready," Tom Weir said unhappily, his small eyes made even smaller by a squint of seriousness.

"You are in command of D Company," Benteen said conversationally. "You couldn't know—you shouldn't know—what goes on in the other companies. That's my job. I admire your bravado, but you have certain responsibilities." He reached across and clapped Weir on the shoulder roughly, though not unaffectionately. "Anytime you have a question, Tom, come and see me. I'll tell you everything I know and more. More than you bargained for, that's for sure."

Benteen laughed abruptly and even homely Tom Weir smiled.

"Don't go off on your own," Benteen repeated. "Check with me."

The smiling white-haired senior captain of the regiment took the lead once again of his three-company battalion and they moved west along the trail toward the Little Big Horn an hour or more behind the rest of the column. The pack train was in chaos.

Sergeant Daniel A. Knipe of Tom Custer's C Company led two "sets of four" beyond the lone tepee in a routine flank-security measure. The lanky, red-headed South Carolina farm boy stopped and stared in amazement. To the northwest—in the vicinity of a cluster of high hills just east of the Little Big Horn—Sergeant Knipe spotted a cluster of Indians, watching the cavalry and apparently headed east—away from the river.

Knipe's report to First Sergeant Edwin Bobo was overheard by Tom Custer's second-in-command, Second Lieutenant Henry Moore Harrington. Harrington was twenty-seven, a West Pointer (class of '72 with Wallace and Varnum), darkly handsome with a black mustache and goatee. He was slightly pudgy, but a month of hardtack and bacon had trimmed him into a lean, hot-eyed cavalryman. Harrington didn't verify Knipe's sighting—a tribute to Knipe's reputation—but rode straight to Tom Custer.

Scar-faced Captain Thomas W. Custer was listening to his older brother explain the misunderstanding with the scouts to Lieutenant Jimmy Calhoun when Harrington rode up. Custer overheard the report and galloped toward Knipe's position to see it for himself. It was there—watching the Indians near the peaks just east of the river—that Lieutenant Varnum found Custer.

"Have you seen the village?" Custer asked at once.

Varnum shook his head, speechless for a time. But his head-shake was of amazement and not a negative reply, as his report confirmed.

"It's just over that line of bluffs there," he said, indicating the high point Custer was now studying with DeRudio's glasses, "and it's the biggest damn village I've ever seen."

"Will Major Reno find it?" Custer wanted to know.

"He can't miss it!"

Custer shook his head. "If a thing is possible, it could happen. And with Major Reno in command, it just might. Go with him. Make sure he finds this village."

He turned to his brother. "Come on, Tom, let's have a look for ourselves."

Major Reno's three-company battalion was trotting rapidly toward a natural ford in the Little Big Horn. Captain Myles Moylan's A Company on black horses was in the lead, but being pressed closely by Captain Thomas H. French's M Company.

Lieutenant William W. Cooke, the adjutant, shouted after them, "For God's sake, men, don't run your horses like that! You will need them in a few minutes."

Some wag—anonymous in the seething mass of men and horseflesh—wondered aloud what the tall Canadian was doing so close to the *fighting* men and so far away from Custer's skirts. Laughter greeted this sally, which Cooke affected not to hear. Myles Keough, the black-bearded Irish soldier of fortune, rode beside him.

At the ford, Reno and Hodgson were surprised to see them.

"We are all going in at the advance," Cooke remarked with a laugh, "and Myles Keough is coming, too!"

The troops laughed at this and its implications and the dark-faced major merely flushed and turned away.

They watered at the ford and seemed hesitant to cross and remarks drifted up and down the broken formations.

"Papa GAC's sent Mama Cookey to make sure Reno finds the ford!"

"And Colonel Keough's gonna show 'em all how to fight!"

First Sergeant John M. Ryan of French's M Company moved in among the men, cautioning them not to let their raillery be overheard by the wrong party or reported.

"Save your wind," he advised, not unkindly.

Lieutenant Carlo DeRudio was one of the first into the water, which was about four feet deep and eighty yards wide at the crossing. His horse splashed water on Major Reno close behind.

"What are you trying to do?" Reno shouted mock-angrily. "Drown me before I am killed?"

They re-formed on the other side by companies in response to the calls by Trumpeter William Hardy of A Company at Lieutenant Hodgson's command. It was the first trumpet the men and horses had heard in three days and they were galvanized. A Company was in the lead of the column of fours when Reno gave the signal to advance and Lieutenant McIntosh's G Company brought up the rear.

The scouts were once more in the lead, racing across the level prairie toward a small herd of ponies to the right of the advancing battalion. They called excitedly to one another as they skillfully cut out the ponies and began driving them east toward the river. Gerard was alerted by their cries and, understanding their language, looked in the direction they had indicated. Some fifty Sioux horsemen were parading their ponies back and forth in front of the advancing column just out of range. Some were dragging bushes tied to their ponies' tails between the Reno battalion and the village, creating a crude but effective smoke screen.

Gerard turned his horse and recrossed the Little Big Horn as quickly as he could, his windburned leathery face peculiarly white. He almost bowled over Lieutenant Cooke.

"Well, Gerard, what is the matter now?" Cooke asked jocularly.

"Hell," the civilian replied grimly, "Custer ought to know this right away. He thinks the Indians are running. He ought to know that they're preparing to fight. I'll go back and inform him."

Cooke held up a gauntleted hand.

"All right, Gerard, rejoin the major," he said with a touch of asperity. "I will go back and report." He turned and trotted in the direction of the lone tepee with Captain Keough. Gerard hesitated and then, with a shrug, recrossed the river.

Major Reno, in giving the command for French's M Company to pull out and join A Company in a parallel-column arrangement, arrived at the same conclusion that had prompted Gerard to turn back. He dispatched his cook—an Irish private named Mitchell from Keough's I Company—back to inform Custer that the Indians were not running.

Mitchell passed a large band of stragglers behind McIntosh's trail company, some of whom were still crossing the river.

"The Indians are coming on!" he shouted in answer to questions, and ignored the imputations to his courage as he hurried across the churned-up ford site and set off in search of Custer.

The ground was barren and reduced to an almost lunar appearance by the overgrazing of Indian ponies. Reno's three companies raised a column of dust that nearly obscured their advance.

Custer was on the forward slope of a large hill overlooking the river. He could see the lower reaches of the Indian encampment, but overhanging high ground to his right obscured the bend in the river some miles downstream. As he sat on his sweat-slick sorrel studying the Reno advance, Private Mitchell joined the five-company column that was halted in a narrow swale just behind the hill.

Mitchell delivered his message to the first officer he saw—Captain Keough.

"We know," Keough replied.

Mitchell rejoined his own company—his message undelivered to Custer.

Custer dropped his glasses and turned to Mitch Bouyer as Cooke joined the small command group that included Tom Custer and two orderlies as well.

"How far downstream is the next suitable ford?" Custer inquired of his half-breed guide.

Bouyer gestured toward the hills where Sergeant Knipe had seen the Indians.

"Behind those hills," he said, "there are two, three of them close together."

"How far?"

Bouyer thought it over.

"Four miles, maybe," he answered slowly.

Cooke reported to Custer.

"Gerard says the Indians are not running, but are preparing to fight," the adjutant said.

Custer looked up as if distracted.

"Yes," he murmured, obviously deep in thought, "I know."

He spurred his sorrel back over the hill and rejoined the waiting command. He took off his buckskin jacket, rolling it up and placing it on the saddle behind him without taking his eyes off the skyline.

The command party, including Mitch Bouyer and four Crows, rejoined the five companies in the swale, and the whole force, in two battalions, began to trot and then gallop north by west, keeping the high ground between them and the Indian camp.

Custer pulled out of his lead position momentarily and waited for his brother Tom to come alongside.

"Send a duty sergeant back to Captain Mac and tell him to bring the packs up behind us as rapidly as he can," he told his scar-faced brother.

Tom Custer cast his eyes up and down the length of the galloping column.

In the background, his older brother shouted, "Boys, hold your horses! There are plenty of them there for all of us."

The column was beginning to spread out alarmingly. Some of the horses were moving faster than others and, with the gallop being the most difficult movement for cavalrymen to control, some raced way ahead of the others. Still others were falling out of formation, unable to keep up the breakneck pace.

Sergeant Knipe passed his friend Sergeant August Finckle—who had dropped out—with a cheerful jibe.

"Go ahead," the German Finckle replied disgustedly. "I vill be along ven my horse he decides to run again."

Knipe's comment and Finckle's reply were overheard by Tom Custer, who motioned Knipe alongside.

"Ride back down the main trail," Tom Custer told the South Carolinian. "Tell Captain McDougall to bring back the packtrain straight across to the high ground." He gestured at the peaks toward which the column was galloping. "If the packs get loose, tell him, 'Don't stop to fix them. Cut them off and come quick.' "

Knipe nodded and wheeled his mount around, heading back in the direction they had come. Tom Custer shouted after him, "And if you see Colonel Benteen, tell him to come on quick. Big Indian village."

Knipe galloped on.

Reno had dispatched a second galloper to Custer—his own striker, McIlhargy—as the three-company battalion crossed a prairie dog village. He re-formed the command at a gallop, placing Moylan's A and French's M on line—more or less. McIntosh's G Company remained in column in the rear.

McIlhargy overtook Custer's command shortly after Knipe left. He reported to Keough and was again told that his gallop was in vain. With the patience of a veteran soldier, he rejoined his own company and followed Custer north by west.

Reno signaled Benny Hodgson to bring G Company up into the line on the right flank. The river coursed away from the prairie at this point and the other two companies were drifting to the left. McIntosh's G Company had no more than wheeled into the position indicated when Reno signaled a halt. The trumpets shrilled halt and the three charging companies rumbled to a dust-scattering stop. Two horses from M Company bolted with their riders still on and headed toward the small washout from which the Indians were emerging and firing at the advancing troops. Sergeant Ryan, a burly redhead with a handlebar mustache, bellowed after them, but the two men, Smith and Turley, could not control their horses and were swept into the Indian camp much against their wills.

The trumpets sounded. Hardy, nearest Reno, started, and the

other trumpeters took up the call for skirmishers. In response to the trumpet calls and prodded by their veteran sergeants, the men of A, G, and M Companies formed a skirmish line within range of the lower end of the Indian village. They counted off quickly in fours. The Number Twos tied the reins of their own mounts to the cheekpieces of the mounts of the Number Threes. The Number Ones tied the reins of their mounts to both horses of the Number Twos and Threes. The Number Fours held on to the reins of their own horses and the Number Threes. In this way, the Number Fours could hold four fractious horses without breaking limbs in the process and free the Number Ones, Twos, and Threes to walk forward and fire their Springfield carbines unhampered by horses.

Move forward and fire they did—wildly. Sergeants pleaded and cursed at them to aim and fire low, but for the first few minutes the excitment of the aborted charge was too strong and they fired blindly into the cloud of dust from which the Indians were emerging. Their shooting added the discharged white smoke of their own black-powder weapons to the dust, added the sharp reports of a hundred guns fired simultaneously to the din of Indians whooping, horses neighing, and sergeants and officers screaming and cursing. The troops began to cheer in the Civil War manner.

"Stop that noise!" Reno bellowed. Benny Hodgson mounted his horse after conferring with the distraught major and galloped over toward M Company's first sergeant, John M. Ryan, who was standing back of the skirmish line at his post between the firing men and restless horses.

Young Sergeant Miles F. O'Hara was shot in the chest. He crumpled.

Ryan was standing over him by the time Hodgson arrived.

"Major wants the woods over there skirmished before we move the horses in," the young adjutant told Ryan breathlessly, gesturing at a large patch of timber—mostly cottonwoods—in a natural bend in the river. "It's okay. I've cleared it with Captain French. He said to tell you to take ten men out of the line and clear those woods."

"All right, sir," Ryan said patiently in an unnaturally quiet voice.

"Who is it?" Hodgson asked, peering down at O'Hara.

"Sergeant O'Hara, sir. He had just re-enlisted."

Hodgson shook his head and remounted his horse. Ryan grabbed men off the line and led them at a trot for the woods. The led horses of all three companies followed.

Lieutenant Wallace of G Company waved his long arms as Ryan and the ten men from M Company, preceding the led horses, raced past.

"Wait!" he shouted. "Where do you think you're going?"

"We're to clear out a patch for the horses over there," Ryan told him, pointing at the timber line not fifty feet away.

"Why M Company?" Wallace wanted to know. "You're the farthest away. We're right next to it."

"The order came from Major Reno," Ryan replied briefly.

Lieutenant DeRudio, near the center of the skirmish line, turned his head and caught a glimpse of something. He peered again. He saw two men sitting on horses watching the battle from atop the high hills to the right front and across the river opposite the village. He recognized the blue shirts, his own glasses, and Lieutenant Cooke's unusual side whiskers.

"Cooke and GAC," he murmured to himself, "they must be goin' to attack from the other side."

"What's that?" Varnum asked. The tall, pinch-faced lieutenant had rejoined A Company when his Indian scouts vanished.

DeRudio pointed toward the prominent peak and Varnum strained his eyes. The scout commander without scouts could see the Gray Horse Troop riding north behind the hills DeRudio pointed to.

Custer and Cooke were studying the skirmish line—but only briefly. They directed their attention to the proposed second ford around the bend in the river. Bouyer had pointed it out and sat glumly looking at the immensity of the village, which was visible for the first time.

Custer didn't seem overawed by the size of the encampment. His attention and DeRudio's field glasses were focused on the contemplated ford site. There were no Indians there to oppose a crossing. All that was visible was a dog and an old woman. The braves seemed to be concentrated at the lower end of the village opposite Reno or off after the immense pony herd in the west. The high ground sloping away to Custer's front obscured some of the village, but from where he sat on his horse he could see no large concentration anywhere near the proposed ford.

He lowered the borrowed glasses and secured them to the front of the blue flannel "fireman's" shirt Libbie Custer had handmade for him. He took off his wide-brimmed white hat and slapped on his thigh and the rump of his horse, causing the sorrel to leap forward.

"Hurrah, boys, we got 'em!" he shouted jubilantly as he raced down the reverse slope of the hill to rejoin the halted five companies. "We caught them napping! We'll go down, make a crossing, and finish them up! Then it's home to station!"

The men cheered wildly and the five companies in a column of fours lunged forward, swerving to the right to enter a narrow cedar-lined coulee on their way down from the height above the Little Big Horn to the unprotected ford site.

Reno's skirmish line advanced less than a hundred yards, firing rather wildly at the large washout immediately ahead of them, from which the Indians were occasionally emerging to return the fire.

On the left flank, the Ree scouts had all but disappeared. Fred F. Gerard stood in a tight little group composed of Charlie Reynolds, Isaiah Dorman, and George Herendeen. Of the soldiers, only Lieutenant Hare, the thin Texan, remained with them—Varnum having returned disgustedly to his company. The civilians took careful aim at Indians prancing their ponies back and forth just out of range. Herendeen and Gerard vied for one particularly spectacular hostile who was working his way in dangerously close. Both their shots fell short, and the Indian scampered back.

The mounted Sioux began to appear in increasing numbers on the left flank from the direction of the high plain just west of the river valley. The led horses were safely in the timber, having been brought without incident down and out of an old river channel— now dry—up past the high ground covered with brush and timber and down in a low pocket lightly forested just north of an open park and south of the winding Little Big Horn. The civilians began to move toward the horses.

Reno noticed the turning movement of the Sioux from the west. Fire along the skirmish line had slackened and the fire from the washout to the front was heavier and more accurate, though only Sergeant O'Hara had been hit.

"Tell Lieutenant McIntosh to flank-right into the timber between the Indians and the horses," Reno instructed Lieutenant Hodgson. He didn't wait for the slight young adjutant to acknowledge, but moved himself toward the left flank of the skirmish line, beckoning Captains Moylan and French and relaying identical instructions to both of them.

A and M Companies moved with alacrity and reached the natural trench formed by the riverbed almost at the same time, though they had the farthest to go. The new skirmish line faced almost at right angles to the old one, and French's M Company, which had been on the left of the old line in the open, was the first into the new position. It took the extreme left and forced the right-flank company—McIntosh's G Company—into a very small area on the right flank of the trench closest to the Indian village. Major Reno crashed through the timber, locating the horses and civilians, while Captain Moylan, with the straight sandy mustache and level blue eyes, took charge of the skirmish line in the old riverbed, directing the fire to the right and front.

Gerard and Reynolds found themselves on a point of high ground just inside the timber behind G Company. They were joined by Lieutenant Varnum, who couldn't stay in one place very long, and Lieutenant Hare, who stayed to sit down and carefully fire his weapon. He tumbled an Indian far out to the front— first blood for the small shooting club joined by Herendeen and Dorman.

Custer's five companies were racing pell-mell down the cedar-lined coulee—away from the river. The narrow defile was so small at points that the column was forced to bunch up in twos rather than fours and their forward progress slackened. Custer pulled out and gestured Trumpeter Martin, the regimental orderly, alongside.

"Orderly, I want you to ride to take a message to Colonel Benteen," he shouted above the din of clattering hooves as he watched the lead company swing to the left and enter the broad coulee that ran east-west and straight at the intended ford. "Ride as fast as you can and tell him to hurry. Tell him it's a big village and I want him to come quick. And tell him to bring the ammunition packs."

Without a backward glance, he left the confused young Italian immigrant and raced toward the head of the column to help sort them back into column formation with Tom Custer's C Company leading.

Martin, dazedly, turned his horse and started back up the draw.

"Wait, orderly," Adjutant Cooke, who had overheard the conversation, called. "I'll give you a message." He pulled his notebook out of his pocket and began to scribble rapidly with a pencil. He tore the message from the book, folded it four ways, and handed it to the baffled messenger.

"Now, orderly," he said slowly and distinctly as the racket of the charging column receded, "ride as fast as you can to Colonel Benteen. Take the same trail we came down. If you have time and there is no danger, come back. Otherwise, stay with your company."

Swarthy, flat-nosed John Martin galloped back up the narrow coulee, not pausing to look back until he got to the top. When he looked back, the five companies were in a column of fours once again and moving rapidly at a trot toward the ford. Tom Custer's C Company on sorrels was in the lead, followed by Yates's F Company. The Gray Horse Troop, under Lieutenant A. E. Smith and Jack Sturgis, was in the middle, followed by Keough's small I Company and Calhoun's L Company.

He turned his horse and raced away as a short, sharp burst of fire exploded from his right rear. A rider was galloping toward him. As he neared, he realized it was the general's younger brother, Bos Custer, who had been with the packs.

"Where is the general?" Boston Custer shouted.

"You will find him in the valley just behind that ridge," Martin replied in his uncertain Italian accent. Young Custer galloped down the cedar-lined coulee and Martin headed back toward the lone tepee.

"Your horse is limping," the youngest Custer informed Martin in parting.

Reno moved half of G Company out of the line through the timber all the way to the river on the other side of the horses. Indians were on the east side of the river now and firing at the horses.

Restless Lieutenant Varnum saw the move and concluded that G Company was leading a probe into the Indian village just north of the small peninsula Reno's three companies were occupying.

"I'm going to charge," he announced.

Reno was standing beside him in an instant.

"I wish you would go back to the line and see how things are," he said with some exasperation. As the hot-blooded scout commander hurried off in the direction indicated, Reno called after him, "Come back and report to me!"

Varnum joined a very cool, collected Myles Moylan, who was walking up and down behind the line coaching the men who were shooting. Varnum calmed down and helped him.

Sergeant Daniel Knipe was in sight of the lone tepee when he encountered the three-company battalion led by Benteen. He barely slowed down, shouting that the packs were urgently needed and that Custer was going to charge. His brief remarks galvanized the Benteen battalion. Weir led out on the left, trotting rapidly. The other two companies followed on the right, with Benteen in the center, way out in front on his long-legged bay.

"We're running out of ammunition," Moylan said quietly to the two officers beside him. "Go back and bring the horses up with a file from each platoon."

The two officers were the frenetic Varnum and a calm DeRudio. They led two groups of A Company men back in search of the horses.

The small group of G Company skirmishers sent back to protect the horses from fire across the river were drawing heavy fire from three sides. DeRudio joined them.

Varnum led the horses back through the timber and around toward the wide-open park on the south side of the little peninsula. Men from all three companies on the firing line slipped back to resupply with ammunition. Lieutenant McIntosh, in the confusion, started back through the underbrush toward the spot where the horses had been until Varnum moved them.

Sergeant Knipe found the packtrain moving slowly but in good order about two miles behind Benteen. Captain McDougall took the hurry-up order calmly. He stopped briefly to separate the ammunition packs from the others and place them in front. He split his own B Company into two platoons—one in front and one in the rear.

"If we get hit," he instructed Lieutenant Mathey and the non-coms, "throw out the rear platoon as skirmishers and let the rest of the packs go. If that doesn't work, we'll circle the ammo packs and wait for help. We may have to eat mule flesh for a while, but we've got enough ammunition to hold off the whole Sioux nation. Stay together. If the packs get loose, don't stop to tighten them. Just let them go. The blankets and bacon are not important now."

The Indians had reached the south end of the little peninsula and had Reno bottled up. Sergeant Ryan on the left flank was the first to notice the fire now coming from all points—including from across the river.

"Captain," he told Tucker French calmly, "the Indians are in our rear."

"Oh, no," French replied distractedly, "those are General Custer's men."

The fire was coming in faster all around, but miraculously, no one had been hit. The Indians were crawling up closer and closer.

Ryan surveyed the situation with a practiced eye.

"The best thing we can do is to cut right through them," he concluded out loud.

Further back among the led horses, Major Reno had come to the same conclusion. He bellowed furiously above the din, but the trumpeters were nowhere to be seen.

"Charge!" The horse holders, the Number Fours, took up the call. "Charge! We are going to charge!"

Being the most experienced men in the ranks, they warned their counterparts in the line that a command had been given though no trumpets had been blown. Their almost frantic calls had a demoralizing effect on the men Myles Moylan had worked so hard to calm. Without waiting for confirmation, the men from A and M Companies left their positions and raced to the horses, frantically searching for their own. Their querulous calls and the responding semi-hysterical shouts of the horse holders rose in a babble of noise that was punctuated by the zip of Indian guns coming closer. The Indians took advantage of the sudden lull in the firing line to work themselves into an almost point-blank range.

Lieutenant McIntosh was still gone looking for horses when Lieutenant Wallace led a small party of ammo bearers back to what had been the line. He found it almost completely deserted and heard the frantic "Charge! Charge!" cries of the horse holders. Wallace hustled what remained of G Company toward the horses.

Major Reno sat on his horse watching the pandemonium that was exploding around him. He eyed the nearing puffs of smoke that showed the Indians moving in closer and closer.

Private Henry Klotzbucher, a German immigrant in M Company, reeled in his saddle and fell screaming horribly, "*Mein Gott!* I am hit!"

Ryan and two other men moved to his side to help him back into his saddle, but he struggled and began to scream piteously.

Reno was watching Bloody Knife, the dour part-Sioux scout, sign his evaluation of the situation. Reno turned away briefly to ascertain the cause of the commotion in M Company. When he turned back, Bloody Knife's head exploded.

Red spray and small gray chunks splattered the major, causing him to pull back in alarm and revulsion.

"Dismount!" he yelled, and those closest to him did so.

A moment's reflection later, Reno was back in the saddle and riding his horse east then south around the open park area through the less dense underbrush toward the open prairie to the south.

M Company, distracted by the loss of Klotzbucher, milled uncertainly and A Company took the lead.

"Any of you men who wish to make your escape, follow me," Reno shouted to the knots of troopers from all three companies who had dismounted and were gazing around in confusion and alarm.

Lieutenant Hodgson, the adjutant, was afoot and shouted at Captain Myles Moylan as the latter rode past.

"Where are you going, Moylan?"

"I am going to charge," Moylan called back over his shoulder.

Lieutenant Varnum overheard the exchange and wailed, "For God's sake, don't leave! There are enough of us here to hold off the whole Sioux nation!"

No one paid any attention to the hatless, frantic chief of scouts as they mounted with almost indecent haste—even bowling over comrades and taking horses that did not belong to them. The Indians were upon them at once.

Varnum screamed, "Company A men, halt! Let us fight them! For God's sake, don't run!"

But A Company thundered past. The civilians looked up in alarm as the horses rushed past them.

"What damn fool move is this?" Fred Gerard demanded.

"I don't know," Lonesome Charlie Reynolds answered quietly. "We will have to go. We will have to get out of this."

He moved toward his horse brushing aside Gerard, who tried to stop him. Gerard looked around accusingly and spotted Captain Moylan trotting past, the branches taking a terrible toll of his uniform and face.

"What do you think you're doing?" the civilian demanded of the Army officer.

"Charge the Indians," Moylan recited.

"We'll have to go out slow," Gerard told him. "We don't understand bugle calls."

A little to the rear of all this, Private Elihu F. Clear, a short, dark Civil War veteran and Lieutenant Hare's orderly, brought a horse for the tall Texan. The two mounted and raced out of the timber together. When Hare looked back, he saw that Clear's saddle was empty. He hesitated momentarily, but a large painted buck was bearing down on him. The Indian reached across to pull the Texan off his horse and Hare shot him in the face. He rode on.

The tail end of Moylan's A Company was still in confusion. Sergeant Stanislas Roy, a short, French-born veteran, yelled at the milling throng.

"Where's my horse?"

Lieutenant Nick Wallace, leading part of G Company, rode past him—his knees practically up to his chin, jockey-style.

"Grab any horse you can find and get out of here!" he yelled. It appeared that he had done just that himself, as the horse he rode was small and plainly terrified.

"Grab any horse you can find!" he repeated to the still-dismounted stay-behinds. "Let's get out of here!"

Custer's five companies—C, E, F, I, and L in two battalions under Keough and Yates—galloped on. Stragglers began to drop out. Two men from Tom Custer's C Company gave up altogether. A short Englishman named James Watson and a ruddy young Scotsman named Peter Thompson found themselves in the rear, kicking exhausted horses impatiently. Watson's horse took the abuse as long as he was going to and suddenly jumped up and trotted away. Watson was then afoot and soon joined by Thompson. They started walking back toward the high ground, encountering men from their own company along the way.

On the northeast side of the small position on the peninsula, Lieutenant Carlo DeRudio was directing the fire of the erstwhile horse guards from G Company. Trumpeter McVeigh from A Company appeared beside him.

"Here is your horse, Lieutenant," he said matter-of-factly.

DeRudio made a gesture of annoyance.

"I do not want my horse," he snapped.

"They are leaving the timber, Lieutenant," McVeigh replied patiently.

DeRudio didn't reply, so McVeigh rode off. After a short exchange with the advancing Indians across the river, DeRudio belatedly mounted his horse. As he rose, he spotted a guidon stuck in the bank of the river. He pointed it out to a fleeing trooper.

"Get that guidon!" he ordered.

"To hell with the guidon!" the soldier shouted back. "Don't you see the Indians are coming in?"

The soldier rode off.

DeRudio dismounted and walked over to the flag. As he reached to pull it out, a volley exploded in his face. He ducked back, but held on to the lance on which the guidon was mounted. He jerked it free. He looked behind him as he remounted. Everyone was gone. But he had the guidon.

Charlie Reynolds rode past a knot of dismounted troopers gathered around George Herendeen. Herendeen called to his fellow guide, "Charlie, don't try to ride out. We can't get away from this timber."

Reynolds looked to the open prairie where Herendeen was pointing. Several hundred mounted Sioux were chasing two pitifully small blue columns racing toward the ford. He took a deep breath and spurred his horse. Just as he broke out of the woods, an Indian fired at him point-blank. Reynolds' horse went down and the doughty plainsman somersaulted to his feet, still clutching his rifle with his good left hand. He was awkwardly trying to work the action with his bandaged right hand when a half dozen near-naked Indians rode him down. Herendeen fired futilely into the cloud of dust the action raised. He then withdrew into the timber.

Private Rapp of G Company was waiting anxiously, holding Lieutenant McIntosh's horse, when the part-Indian company commander strode nonchalantly back. A sharp volley from the dried-up riverbed the battalion had used as a trench killed Rapp, and the two horses he was holding broke away, leaving McIntosh afoot. The phlegmatic McIntosh made his way deeper into the timber.

A little further on he encountered a handful of his own men. One of them, Private Samuel McCormick, a brown-haired, ruddy-faced Irishman, handed his commander the reins to his own horse.

"Take it, Lieutenant," he urged. "We're all going to die here anyway."

McIntosh mechanically took the reins, and when he turned from restraining the excited horse to calm the enlisted man, he found himself alone. He mounted and rode out, carefully avoiding the trench.

Lieutenant DeRudio encountered Benny Hodgson leading a limping horse. He dismounted and examined the animal, oblivious to the hail of lead around him.

"Nothing," he reported perplexedly. "Maybe a spent round."

Hodgson mounted and led the limping horse out into the open. DeRudio headed deeper into the woods toward the river.

Moylan's A Company was running hard in a column of fours led by Major Reno and Captain Moylan. They swung to their left to avoid a very large mounted party of Sioux who had blocked off the way to the ford. Captain French, leading M Company on their right, swung to his left to prevent them from being split apart by the whooping Indians. Lieutenant Wallace was leading part of G Company in a mass behind. Lieutenant McIntosh was gaining on them, firing his pistol at the veritable swarms of Indians who were pressing in from the right and rear. The Indians were attempting to throw troopers off their horses and count coup by touching them with long coup sticks and hatcheting and spearing those who wouldn't fall.

Three men toward the rear of the right-flank company, French's M, fell victim to the Indians' buffalo-running tactics—including Dan Newell's good friend Henry Cody, alias Scollin. Newell himself was painfully wounded in the left thigh. He swayed in his saddled, but hung on. Five other members of the exposed right flank were hit—including the Swiss Private Braun, who was hit in the thigh and hatcheted in the face, but managed to stay ahorse.

A Company was riding through heavy fire from the opposite side of the river where the Indians had worked themselves when Reno withdrew into the timber. These same Indians were now racing along the east bank, pouring shots into the nearest soldiers —A Company. Moylan's Forty Thieves were in good order until they reached the river.

There, at the new ford site chosen because of the pressure from the Indians on the prairie and clutched at desperately by the frantic column, A Company was not faring well. The banks were steep and soft. The water was up to the horses' necks. There was an ill-defined buffalo trail leading to the water's edge and away from the opposite bank. But it was narrow—damned narrow. A and M Companies bunched up and the Indian marksmen and daring coup counters, sensing weakness, swarmed in close for the kill.

A Company lost seven men in less than two minutes. During the same time, four men were wounded—two from the right and two from the fire on the left. The crossing was a shambles—literally every man for himself.

The five companies under Custer's immediate command galloped west toward the mouth of the coulee and the ford site located there. Tom Custer's C Company on sorrels led the way a short distance behind Cooke and the regimental commander, the two color sergeants, and the scouts with Mitch Bouyer. Behind C Company galloped the bays of George Yates's F Company, whose heavy bodies, shiny with sweat, carried the dust-covered members of the once crack Band Box Troop. The gray horses of E Company were next, led by cripple-armed Algernon E. Smith. The two trail companies followed at some distance—Keough's "Wild I" and Jim Calhoun's L Company, both mounted on bays.

Mitch Bouyer signed to the four Crow scouts: "You should go now. You have done what was expected of you. Go now. There is no use for you to die."

The three older ones needed no prompting and whipped their ponies away in the direction Trumpeter Martin had taken minutes before. The youngster, Curley, hesitated.

"Go on," Bouyer signed to him. "You had better leave now before we are all cleaned out." He pointed to the rough hills in the east and Curley, in a daze, trotted away.

George Herendeen emerged from the timber a second time and, glancing around suspiciously, began to ride out. He hadn't gone thirty feet when his horse flopped over—victim to a well-aimed Sioux bullet. As he dashed back into the timber, he glanced around to see several Indians walking toward a badly wounded Isaiah Dorman. The Negro was screaming pitifully in Sioux. He screamed once again—a long-drawn-out, unintelligible yell that was understood universally. As Herendeen turned his eyes away from the gory finish of Dorman, he spotted Lieutenant Donald

McIntosh afoot, firing two pistols with icy calm. There were at least twenty Sioux surrounding him and closing in to within pistol range to finish him.

A dark-haired German private in M Company named Roman Rutten noticed McIntosh's predicament. Rutten's horse was unused to his rider and badly spooked by the Indians. With Rutten unable to do much more than hang on grimly, the horse bolted through the middle of the Indians surrounding McIntosh on the prairie about halfway from the timber to the hasty ford site. McIntosh grabbed at a stirrup of the passing horse, but missed. The Indians swarmed over him. Rutten emerged unscathed and reached the ford a minute later. He tried to turn his horse around, but the horse was having nothing to do with the Indians. Rutten looked over his shoulder agonizingly and watched the tall half-breed lieutenant stagger with a shot to the chest. Rutten turned back around in shock and rode on.

Lieutenant Hodgson was among the last to leave the timber, but his limping horse outran most of G Company strung out behind the double column in a mass. As he passed Nick Wallace, he called out anxiously, "What is this? A retreat?"

"Most damnably like a rout!" Wallace replied as he fired his pistol at a coup-seeking Indian who got too close.

Hodgson rode on.

Varnum, on a thoroughbred, outdistanced the rest of the fleeing troopers and arrived at the head of the column just as it was abruptly halted at the riverbank.

"Where are you running to?" the hatless scout commander demanded. "Dismount, skirmishers! This is no way to charge!"

Another hatless officer was suddenly beside him, nearly bowling Varnum over in getting to the river's edge.

"I am in command here, sir!" Major Reno barked.

The astonished Varnum noted that Captain Moylan was right beside Reno—head down and aiming his horse at an incredibly narrow spot in the splashing confusion of the ford.

Varnum's orderly, Private Elijah Strode, was hit in the right ankle and swayed in his saddle. Varnum steadied him and led Strode's horse into the river. Varnum's own horse swam the river without seeming to break stride and mounted the far bank in one tremendous jump. Varnum slid off the rump and landed on his feet. He stood on the far bank with two pistols in his hands blazing away, while tears of frustration and fury coursed down his unshaven cheeks. He swore loudly and fluently and fired without aiming.

George Armstrong Custer's right arm went up imperiously and the column came to a dust-scattering halt. Horses snorted and pawed the ground. It was all the soldiers could do to keep them in one place. The officers trotted forward for a conference.

Gaunt-faced, long-haired Boston Custer arrived just as Calhoun and one-eyed J. J. Crittenden joined the officers' call. Bos shook hands with his brother Tom dramatically. Their older brother was studying the west end of the ravine with DeRudio's glasses.

"It's a big village all right," Custer said in an unnaturally level voice that nonetheless carried sharply above the noise of the restless horses and murmuring officers. He dropped the glasses and secured them to the front of his blue flannel shirt. "George," he told Captain Yates, "your three companies will go in with me—across the ford in line or as best we can manage. We'll re-form on the far bank and sweep through the village."

Yates nodded stolidly and Custer's flashing blue eyes lit on Captain Myles W. Keough.

"Colonel Keough," he told the black-bearded Irishman, "your two companies will remain in column and swing north once you reach the ford. Take Bouyer with you. He will show you another ford north of here. Cross there and bag anything that gets away."

He looked back down the ragged column.

"Keep your troops well in hand," he told all the officers, who then trotted back to their respective commands, leaving the three Custer brothers in front with Lieutenant Cooke and the two color sergeants. Custer paced his white-stockinged sorrel in a tight arc impatiently.

After an interminable pause, he faced west and brought his arm up. Sergeant Hughes, the middle-aged Irishman who carried the red-and-blue battle flag of Custer's own design, lifted the nine-foot lance into the air. It fluttered momentarily and then dropped. The five companies surged forward.

Trumpeter John Martin's gray horse was limping so badly that the most the little Italian could coax out of him with spurs was a pathetic, staggering walk. Captain Fred Benteen spotted him about a half mile away and threw up his right hand in a peremptory signal to halt.

Martin reached the white-haired senior captain and handed him the message written by adjutant Cooke. Benteen unfolded it slowly and scowled at it in silence. Martin's horse wouldn't stand still. At length, Benteen looked up.

"Where is General Custer now?" he demanded.

"About three miles from here—"

"Is he under attack or what?"

"Yes," Martin replied uncertainly, "being attacked."

Benteen sighed noisily and looked disgusted.

"Where is the general now?" he repeated.

"In the village. The Indians . . ." Martin screwed up his face in concentration as he struggled to word his message in English. "They asleep."

Benteen looked askance as Captain Tom Weir rode up to see what was going on. Benteen wordlessly handed Weir the note.

"The general charge and they run," Martin contributed brightly.

Benteen stared at the young immigrant trumpeter.

"What's the matter with your horse?"

"He just tired out, I guess," Martin replied with an embarrassed laugh.

"Tired out?" Benteen said loudly. "Look at his hip."

Martin dismounted and saw the bloody wound in the horse's rump. As he turned, both Weir and Benteen could see the splashed blood on Martin's back.

"You're lucky it was the horse and not you," Benteen said kindly as Godfrey and Edgerly rode up to join the conference.

Benteen looked up and down the trail. He read the message aloud in a perplexed tone of voice.

" 'Benteen. Come on. Big Village. Be quick. Bring Packs. W. W. Cooke. P.S. Bring Pacs.' "

"Well," he said at last, "if he wants me to hurry, how does he expect that I can bring the packs?"

The other three officers stared at him wordlessly.

"If I am going to be of service to him," Benteen concluded, "I think I had better not wait for the packs."

Without another word, he swung his horse around and led out in the direction the main column had taken an hour before. The three companies—H, D, and K—followed at a rapid trot.

G Company, at the tail of the mass of men and horses struggling to cross the river, suffered badly. Nine men were unhorsed as they raced toward the river. The Indians moved in among them, swinging hatchets and lances with bloody abandon. Two corporals and a sergeant died trying to extricate men from desperate one-sided hand-to-hand duels on horseback with the exhilarated Sioux.

The first sergeant of G Company, Edward Botzer, died trying to fight a lonely rear guard at the ford against three Indians who swarmed in from three different directions. Horses slammed into each other and men reeled in their saddles and the survivors clung grimly to their own reins and saddle cantles, too numbed by the slaughter to fight back. The Indians screamed in triumph with each fallen trooper, calling attention to the coups they struck and adding further to the mad confusion in the cavalry ranks.

Lieutenant Benny Hodgson's horse floundered in the water and, seconds later, the soaked young adjutant emerged from the river holding a badly wounded thigh. Horses crashed past him at breakneck speed even in the water. He was buffeted by the water thrown at him and the nearness of the lunging thousand-pound animals.

"For God's sake," he screamed, "don't leave me!"

Charles "Bounce" Fischer, a young German immigrant who served as trumpeter in M Company, heard the cry of the popular young officer and removed his boot from his left stirrup and kicked it out as he splashed past Hodgson. The officer grabbed the free stirrup and was towed across the river by Bounce Fischer's horse. On the far side, the sudden jolt of the firm ground on his wounded leg caused him to shriek wordlessly and release the stirrup. Fischer attempted to turn around, but his horse was panicked by the others thundering past and lunged ahead despite Fischer's frantic sawing on the reins.

Hodgson limped out of the way of another horse and stood to one side, backing up painfully on one good leg and attempting to fire his pistol. An Indian rifle shot nearly exploded his thin chest and he flopped over backward and lay still. The horses continued to rumble past his dead body.

Captain Tucker French was fighting a one-man rear guard on the far side of the ford well to the right of the oncoming horses. He was dismounted, his horse's reins held by Reno's orderly, Private Edward Davern. French fired his heavy .50-caliber Springfield hunting rifle as fast as he could reload.

"We must go back over and cover for the wounded," Davern yelled to him above the din. Opposite the two men, three G Company privates were unhorsed with a wail of panic and a corresponding shriek of triumph from the victorious Indians.

"I'll try, I'll try," French yelled distractedly as he continued to fire. He shot one heavyset Indian out of the saddle at about a hundred yards and delayed reloading while he watched his victim thrash on the riverbank opposite. French's coal-black eyes glowed.

Lieutenant Hare rode toward the high bluff just to the left of the crossing where Custer had sat surveying the valley not more than an hour before. A shout from behind him caused him to turn his head. Men behind him were waving frantically and pointing at the top of the hill, which he could not see. He turned his horse around and headed for the top of the neighboring hill on the right-hand side of the crossing. He saw the men below still gesturing and shouting incoherently and turned his head.

Assistant Surgeon James DeWolf in his occupational linen duster flopped at the base of the hill. Two privates from M Company, who had followed, died nearly beside him. One was shot in the neck and the other died horribly with a Sioux arrow through the eye.

Hare rode his horse up the other hill. He passed a tall, weeping Lieutenant Varnum, who was firing his pistols as rapidly as he could and shouting.

"For God's sake, men, don't run!" he wailed. "There are a good many officers and men killed and wounded and we've got to go back and get them!"

Hare didn't notice anyone paying much attention to the tall scout commander.

Benteen was coming toward the first ford at a gallop. The trail his three-company battalion was following suddenly split. He threw up his right hand in a signal to halt. Weir, Godfrey, and the other two lieutenants joined him at once. The older man gestured at the parting of trails.

"Here we have the two horns of a dilemma," he began.

Off to his right, he noticed a clump of Indians driving a small herd of ponies. He drew his pistol, cocked it, and swerved in their direction. He was almost on top of them before he recognized them as Ree scouts.

"Otoe Sioux!" They informed him in chorus. "Heap Sioux!"

They gestured and mimed the act of firing carbines and kept jabbering, "Pooh, pooh," and "Otoe Sioux." Benteen looked beyond them and saw the tail of Reno's column under heavy attack at the other ford. The victorious Sioux were now swinging out in a widening circle and continuing to pour a murderous fire into the stragglers. Benteen's three companies thundered up behind him.

And then it happened. A few scattered shots from the west bank of the Little Big Horn was all the opposition Custer and his column encountered. But one of the shots hit Custer—high on the torso on the left side. Vic, his white-stockinged sorrel, reared involuntarily and the commander of the 7th Cavalry swayed in the saddle. Sergeant John Vickory, the tall dark Canadian who carried the blue regimental colors, reached over and grabbed the trailing reins, while side-whiskered Lieutenant Cooke grabbed Custer from the opposite side holding on to his shirt collar at the nape of his neck.

The three companies immediately behind Custer swung into a sort of line and when the cry "The general's hit!" went up, they halted uncertainly. Further back, Keough halted I and L Companies, still in column.

The three companies behind the fallen Custer milled uncertainly. George Yates and Tom Custer trotted forward. Cooke shouted above the crack of Indian rifles and the snorting and general hubbub of the confused cavalrymen and their horses.

"Doctor! Doctor!" he yelled. "Fetch Dr. Lord!"

Frail, bespectacled Dr. George Lord hurried forward. Sergeant Vickory and Lieutenant Cooke guided the skittish horse and its stricken rider through the impromptu line formed by Yates's battalion. Troopers strained to see what was going on.

"Skirmishers!" Tom Custer shouted at a befuddled George Yates. "Throw out a line!"

Lieutenant A. E. Smith took charge and shouted at Trumpeter Thomas McElroy, a ruddy-faced Civil War vet. McElroy began to blow and the other trumpeters took up the call. The Number Fours in each set held the reins of the other three horses in the peculiar cavalry drill, and the other three in the sets, thus freed, jogged forward—carbines at the ready. They began to fire sporadically across the river into the village.

Lieutenant DeRudio, deep in the timber, heard a cry of alarm. He crawled forward to investigate and noticed the Indians heading back toward the village as fast as their horses could run. He looked up at the bluff Reno had retreated to and saw Benteen's three-company column riding up at a gallop. The fire died almost abruptly, as the Indians seemed almost to vanish.

Dr. Henry R. Porter, the fine mustachioed surgeon, found himself at the top of the hill beside Major Reno. Reno was silent—staring dully at the foot of the steep hill where the Indians were precipitately breaking off the slaughter. His high dark forehead was covered by a red bandanna which effectively kept his lank dark hair out of his eyes, but gave him a rather piratical look.

Dr. Porter, harried by the hysterical calls for medical attention, spoke briefly and bluntly.

"Major, the men were pretty demoralized by the rout, weren't they?"

Reno eyed the young doctor coldly.

"No," he said icily. "That was a cavalry charge, sir."

Captain Moylan was forming the retreating cavalrymen into a skirmish line of sorts when the clatter and drumming of hooves were first heard above the diminishing sounds of the fight below.

Reno looked up with animation and then ran toward the oncoming soldiers.

Moylan didn't seem to notice the new arrivals, but he acknowledged the sudden presence of Captain French and briefly, monosyllabically, coordinated the forming of a new skirmish line.

George Armstrong Custer lay on the ground behind Yates's led horses as Captain Keough galloped up. Tom Custer and William Cooke stood over him, getting in the way of Dr. Lord, who was trying to cut off the regimental commander's blue flannel shirt.

"Make room!" they both shouted at the others who were crowding in—while they themselves crowded forward anxiously. At last, Cooke wheeled away, bumping into Keough blindly.

"Heart shot," he said in a too calm voice.

Keough squeezed the tall Canadian's shoulder.

"For Christ's sake, do something!" young Lieutenant Jack Sturgis shouted from the front, where his own Gray Horse Troop on the left of the line was being subjected to increasingly steady fire from across the river. Shots were now splattering in from the left flank as Indians swarmed across the river under the cover of the high bluffs to the south of the ford site.

Captain Tom Custer tore himself away from the knot around the fallen leader to take charge. He scanned the terrain.

"North!" he commanded, gesturing toward a long ridge that ran parallel to the river about a half mile east. "We'll swing around the flank! Where's Bouyer?"

The burly, calfskin-vested half-breed trotted over.

"Show us!" Tom Custer commanded.

Bouyer nodded and mounted his horse in one lithe motion. He galloped northwest. The skirmish line fell back as four trumpeters blew the Rally raggedly.

"How does it look?" Tom Custer demanded of the harassed surgeon, Dr. Lord.

"He's gone," Sergeant Vickory answered in a voice of panic. Boston Custer was crying.

Myles Keough found his voice at last.

"Move your people out of here," he told Tom Custer. "I'll cover you from the high ground." He pointed to the steep bluff immediately behind the ragged skirmish line.

Tom Custer nodded dazedly and stumbled blindly toward his horse.

The E Company horse holders began to scream. "Lieutenant Smith! Lieutenant Smith!"

Keough glanced back over his shoulder as he swung into the saddle. The stocky, cripple-armed commander of the Gray Horse

Troop had fallen. Several panicky troopers gathered around him uncertainly.

Sergeant Frederick Hohmeyer, a well-tanned, blond-haired German immigrant and the first sergeant of E Company, bulled his way forward, losing his black campaign hat in the process. He lifted the fallen troop commander and, with the help of two others, draped him over the saddle of his own horse. Lieutenant Jack Sturgis hurried over, leading Lieutenant Smith's horse. Sergeant Hohmeyer took the reins of Smith's horse and spoke calmly, quietly to the young West Pointer.

"You're in charge now, Lieutenant," he said.

The three companies—now under Captain Tom Custer—rode almost due north at a slow trot. With each step their horses took, the Indian fire became heavier and heavier. They rode along the ridge of the high ground nearest the river, but the Indians were pressing in from the west and south with each step. Soon the intended route was abandoned to the unseen Indian snipers and bowmen.

The Indians swarmed across the Little Big Horn at all points and dismounted their ponies to creep up behind the sagebrush and harass the retiring cavalrymen. Bullets zipped and arrows whirred. The progress of the three companies hastened perceptibly.

In the rear, E Company (the Gray Horse Troop) was faring badly. Private Rees, the tallest man in the company, suddenly lurched in his saddle and Sergeant Frederick Hohmeyer lunged for him but missed. Rees fell heavily to the ground, an arrow buried deep in the nape of his neck—so deep that Hohmeyer saw the bloody point sticking out of the tall private's throat like an obscene tongue.

"Dismount!" Hohmeyer shrieked.

A few of the men started to tie the reins of their horses to the cheekpieces of others and Hohmeyer stopped them with a loud cry that could be heard almost all the way to the front of the column.

"No! Dammit! Hold your own horses!"

There was a little uncertainty in the ranks, but the veterans and other sergeants soon showed the confused ones what was expected. They grabbed the reins of their own horses and fired over the backs and rumps with their pistols—trying ever to keep their horses between themselves and the Indians.

Inevitably, the horses were hit. They reared and trumpeted wildly as bullets and arrows found their marks. Some fell heavily, dragging their holders down with them. The men who lost horses were up in a bound, firing wildly in the direction of the Indian fire and scrambling toward the head of the column.

F Company and C Company followed the example of necessity set by the trail company and dismounted, leading their skittish horses and firing over them blindly. The Indians had swarmed across the river in large numbers and threatened to head off the northerly progress of the three beleaguered companies. The three companies drifted down the slope of the hill into a ravine heading in an easterly direction. The Indians took the high ground to the west of them and sent a steady stream of arrows at them.

The arrows arced high and found their marks even though the cavalrymen were all but hidden by their big grain-fed horses. One young private from C Company screamed and fell with an arrow sticking straight down through the top of his skull. It had gone through his black hat.

Tom Custer waved at Lieutenant Cooke and the small party still mounted around General Custer's body. He signaled north—high ground. Cooke began to trot, tugging the reins of the horse that carried his fallen commander. Tom Custer swung around and trotted down the column in full view of the sniping Indians. Arrows whooshed past him, but he remained erect, shouting.

"Let's get up on the high ground. They're murdering us down here. Never mind the man in front of you! Right flank, ho!"

The three companies turned as one and started up the slope of the long narrow ridge that ran north-south generally, less than a mile from the river. One man from F Company fell with an arrow through the leg. His horse skittered away. Tom Custer rode over to where he lay and placed himself and his own horse between the unfortunate trooper and the Indians. He signaled two horseless troopers.

"Carry him! Don't leave him behind. Carry him up the hill."

He fired his pistol impressively, but ineffectually, at the Indians on the heights above him. He seemed to ignore the bullets and arrows that sailed past him. As the two designated troopers carried their burden awkwardly up the hill, Tom Custer rode behind them, circling his own now frantic horse in tight circles to protect their rear.

The Indians seemed emboldened by the abandonment of the ravine and swarmed into it, pouring a galling fire into the struggling column now above them on the slope. Captain George Yates galloped forward to catch up with Cooke, Dr. Lord, and the lifeless body of George Armstrong Custer.

Benteen had barely holstered his pistol when the red-bandannaed Major Reno ran out in front of his horse shrieking at him. Reno's customary stentorian voice had risen several octaves in near hysteria.

"For God's sake, Benteen, halt your command and help me!" he demanded. "I've lost half my men."

Benteen's hand had gone up, signaling the halt, and, without replying to Reno at once, he deployed his three companies in a line covering the east and south slopes of the hill Reno was standing on.

"Where's Custer?" he inquired curtly of Reno.

"I don't know," Reno answered almost petulantly. "He went off downstream and I haven't seen or heard anything of him since."

Benteen looked from the disheveled major to the milling crowd that Moylan was forming into a line. Varnum was weeping with helpless frustration. Benteen looked stern and dismounted slowly, giving his reins to Trumpeter Martin, who had been given another mount of his own. Benteen slowly unfolded the note from Cooke and handed it to Reno without comment.

Reno read and reread it.

"Well," he said querulously at last, "I have lost half my men and I could do no better than I have done."

"Who's lost?" Benteen wanted to know.

"I don't know," Reno told him tightly. "Benny was hit down there. I haven't seen McIntosh or DeRudio." He seemed to be thinking. "I saw Mr. Hare a moment ago. I'll need an adjutant . . ." He handed the note back to Benteen. "Benny was killed," he repeated, "and Bloody Knife and I don't know how many men. Custer was supposed to support me with the whole outfit."

"Well," Benteen replied matter-of-factly, "we'll have to make a junction with him as soon as possible."

Reno blinked rapidly and then nodded. He pivoted and strode back toward Moylan's ragged skirmish line.

"We have assistance now," he announced somewhat shrilly, "and we will go and avenge the loss of our comrades."

The men who heard him cheered, but further down the line the cheering was a little flat.

One of the new arrivals, Lieutenant Ed Godfrey of K Company, dismounted and slowly walked in the direction of Moylan and his men. He studied the valley floor with his intent, eaglelike gaze and saw a small party of Sioux bent over a fallen trooper halfway between the ford and the timber. With almost slow-motion deliberateness, he lifted his carbine to a 45-degree angle and fired a single shot. Incredibly, the round landed a few feet away from the Indians, who were occupied in stripping and scalping. They fled.

Lieutenant Luther Hare saw the shot and joined in the ragged cheer that followed. He walked toward the spot where it had come from and came face to face with his own stern-visaged company commander, Godfrey. He smiled broadly and unrestrainedly pumped his superior's hand.

"We've had a big fight in the bottom," he reported emotionally, "got whipped like hell and I am damned glad to see you!"

Godfrey smiled tightly and clapped the young Texan affectionately on the shoulder.

The only first sergeant present for duty on the hilltop from Reno's battalion was steady John M. Ryan from French's M Company. He checked the muster roll and called out names.

"Sergeant Carey?" he called. There was no answer. After a long pause, a young private answered hysterically.

"He's dead! Sergeant Carey's dead!"

"He's not dead," Ryan replied calmly. "I saw him a few minutes ago. Take it easy, boy." He looked up and down the ragged line. Many of the men were sitting and staring dully at the valley floor. He lifted up his voice again.

"Sergeant Carey! Where are you?"

"He's with the wounded," Private James Weeks, a tall Canadian, informed the first sergeant.

"No, he's not!" someone else shouted.

"Answer to your own names," Ryan admonished sternly, and went on down his muster roll.

Captain Moylan took the A Company muster roll from the wounded Sergeant Heyn and told the husky German to lie back and take it easy. He strolled down the line until he came to blond-haired, blue-eyed Sergeant Burke.

"I want you to act as first sergeant until I find what has happened to Culbertson," Moylan told the Irish Burke. "Call the roll. Heyn's been wounded. Find out who else has been shot and mark it beside their name."

Burke hesitated and then, in a subdued manner, went up and down the line checking off names.

Benteen watched the proceedings dispassionately. He looked back at the three companies he had brought up and nodded. A frown replaced his almost omnipresent grin.

"Where the hell is Custer?" he wondered out loud.

Others were saying the same thing.

"Where has Custer gone to?"

"He's gone off and left us."

"Where the hell is Custer?"

"It's the Washita all over again."

Captain Myles Keough had gained the height to the south of the struggling three-company column that Yates, Tom Custer, and Cooke were leading in a generally north-by-west direction. He halted his company and Lieutenant Jim Calhoun's L Company. The two companies formed a standard skirmish line with three men of each set of four freed to fire their carbines while the horses were held by the Number Fours.

"Aim!" Lieutenant J. J. Crittenden, the infantry officer, called. "Don't waste shots on dust!"

The men fired wildly and erratically nonetheless. Tall, whiskered Sergeant Frank Varden of I Company and short, balding Sergeant James Butler of L Company walked the ragged skirmish line directing fire and, after a time, succeeded in slowing the rate of fire.

From where he sat, still mounted, Captain Keough could see the Indians dashing across the river. They seemed to be concentrated on the left and rear of the retreating column below. Some of the Indians were working their way up the sides of the steep ridge where Keough's two companies had halted. They took advantage of every blade of the foot-high grass and zigzagged their way upward—closer and closer.

"This way!" buckskinned Lieutenant James E. Porter shouted, leading one platoon of I Company to the south rim of the ridge. Under his watchful eye, they began directing a steady aimed fire at the Indians working their way up the ridge from the south. The Indians slowed perceptibly, but kept coming.

Other Indians were working their way up the high ridge to the north and west too. Sergeant Varden took what remained of I Company to the west rim and set up a steady, but largely ineffective fire at the crawling Indians. The Indians kept coming. They kept low to the ground and slithered in a zigzag manner closer and closer.

Lieutenant Calhoun trotted over to Keough.

"We'll have to make a junction with the others," he said with incredible calmness. "The reds are getting between us."

Keough cast an anxious eye south toward the direction they had come. The coulee below was filled with Indians and more were coming across the river. The peaks where General Custer had stopped before dispatching Trumpeter Martin obscured vision in the direction of the back trail.

"Where the hell is Benteen and the packs?" he asked.

Calhoun glanced briefly at the direction they had come and then looked back at the three companies hurrying toward the high point at the north end of the opposite ridge. The higher south end of the ridge almost obscured them to view.

"We're going to lose sight of them," he said calmly.

From the west rim of the ridge, Sergeant Varden shouted a warning. The two company commanders looked in the direction indicated. Large numbers of mounted Indians were gathering to the north of the other ridge—the ridge Tom Custer and the others were riding on.

"Sweet Jesus!" Keough breathed.

"We've got to warn them," Calhoun said.

Keough rode the roughly formed L his skirmishers had made with Calhoun's. When he returned, he stood in his saddle and shouted.

"Now!" he yelled. "Now!"

With each yell, every carbine in the two companies fired as one. The result was two loud crashes that carried over the din of the battle below them.

"Jesus Christ, Wallace, did you hear that?" Lieutenant Charles Varnum demanded of Lieutenant Nick Wallace. "And that?"

Far to the northwest, two distinct crashing volleys rang out. The troops on the hill with Reno stopped talking and listened, straining to hear.

"Hear that?" Captain Myles Moylan asked Captain Thomas French, as the two company commanders huddled, discussing the control of the skirmish line that was no longer apparently needed. "What do you think?"

"I suppose that's Custer—at the other end of the village," French replied with only fractional hesitation. He turned and left Moylan for his own company without another word.

Lieutenant Ed Godfrey, a trifle hard of hearing himself, heard the two crashes, but not trusting his own auditory senses, asked Lieutenant Luther Hare standing beside him, "Did you hear that volley?"

"Yes," Hare replied, "I heard two distinct volleys."

Silver-haired Fred Benteen never stopped smiling. He heard the murmuring comments of the enlisted men as he walked the line. He stopped and listened for a few seconds and then walked on, his smile unaltered.

Lieutenant Win Edgerly and his company commander, Tom Weir, were in conference with two or three of the senior noncoms of D Company. Reno's orderly, Davern, was standing a few feet away from them on an incline above them.

"That must be Custer fighting down in the bottom," Davern announced.

The D Company leadership turned as one to see who had hazarded this guess and then looked themselves to the north. Nothing was visible beyond the high peaks where Custer had stopped for the second time less than an hour before.

"Yes," Captain Weir said quietly at last, his deep-set eyes glowing, "I believe it is."

In the deepest part of the timber in the valley, they heard it too. Lieutenant DeRudio had linked with Fred Gerard and a young half-breed Blackfoot named Billy Jackson. The somewhat ruffled Italian dandy had found a young private from G Company, Thomas F. O'Neill, wandering through the brush and had taken him under his wing. The four men froze—electrified.

"By God, that's Custer comeeng," DeRudio said in an unconscious imitation of Benteen's deep voice. "Let's go and join heem."

Gerard held up a calloused hand. "Let's wait until they come closer," he advised, "until they come opposite us."

Tom Custer heard the volleys. The lead element of the three companies had just reached a level knoll west of the north end of the long ridge. F Company deployed on the north slope of the hill, C Company deployed on the west slope, and E Company threw out a skirmish line in a generally southerly direction.

"What was that all about?" Tom Custer demanded of whiskered Lieutenant Cooke as the two joined Captain George Yates and the three scanned the back trail for signs of Captain Keough.

The big Canadian adjutant's shoulders were heaving from exertion and his dark face was wet with sweat as he took off his white hat and wiped his brow with a cavalry bandanna.

"I suppose he caught sight of Benteen and was giving the old man something to guide on," he said quietly.

The three men—Tom Custer, Yates and Cooke—drifted over toward where Dr. Lord was bent over the prone body of Lieutenant A. E. Smith. General Custer's booted feet stuck out from under a blue Army horse blanket; the men averted their eyes.

An enlisted man who had overheard their conversation shouted to a comrade further down the slope.

"Colonel Benteen's coming!"

The men cheered and took up the cry.

Tom Custer was pale-faced and grim, his bullet scar a red blemish on his otherwise livid cheeks. All along the three skirmish lines arrows and bullets were finding their marks. The Indians were creeping closer. Now and then one would dash forward slung over the side of a pony and touch one of the skirmishers. With a shout of triumph, he would zigzag away, impervious to the shots and curses that pursued him. In the ravines to the west, the Indians massed.

"We'll have to attack them," Tom Custer told George Yates, who nodded numbly.

Tom Custer sprang into the saddle of his skittish horse and galloped down the slope toward E Company. He beckoned grimy, sweating Lieutenant Jack Sturgis over.

"Push them away," he instructed. "Form your people into a regular skirmish line and move toward those ditches as fast as your led horses can keep up with you."

"Take the horses?" Sturgis yelled.

Tom Custer nodded grimly.

"You'll need the ammunition."

"Custer is engaged and we ought to get down there," Weir told big Win Edgerly.

Edgerly nodded. "I think so too," he said calmly.

Weir started up the incline and stopped opposite Davern. He began to pace impatiently. Edgerly and the two remaining sergeants strained to see the ground to the northwest, the direction from which the volleys had come. Suddenly, a thin but distinct cloud of dust lifted over the area about four miles away.

"That must be General Custer," Edgerly concluded to First Sergeant Michael Martin, a fair-haired, middle-aged Irishman who had fought with distinction in the Civil War. "I guess he is getting away with them."

"Yes, sorr," Martin replied in his thick brogue, "and I'm t'inkin' we ought to go down there."

Major Reno had calmed down considerably by the time the volleys were heard on the hill. He was pacing in shorter steps and looking to the south and east. "Where are those packs?" he muttered out loud.

The packs at that moment were encountering the eastward-fleeing Rees who had directed Benteen to Reno's position. They were driving the captured ponies as fast as they could.

"Whole Sioux nation over in valley there," they shouted to a much relieved McDougall, who had recognized them as non-hostiles only seconds before.

"Going back to Powder River," they told the packtrain and escort commander.

Myles Keough led I and L Companies off the high ground into the deep gully that separated his former position from the long north-south ridge the other three companies were on. The Indians before them scattered but closed in to pour harassing fire into the flanks. Sergeant Butler was the first to fall, pincushioned by arrows before the last of L Company even got off the high ridge. The rear of L Company, which Butler had been covering, began to scatter in panic.

"Dismount and fire over your horses!" Keough yelled as he rode back down the disintegrating column. He repeated his instructions frequently, but the troopers needed little urging to dismount from their exposed positions.

Reaching the high ground on the extreme south end of the long ridge at last, Lieutenant Calhoun ordered J. J. Crittenden to throw out a skirmish line to keep the Indians down. The Indians were firing from ravines behind, below, and to all sides of the beleaguered two-company column.

One platoon of L Company deployed, firing steadily at the constantly moving Indians. The pressure eased somewhat and Keough turned and rode north to the front.

Still in the timber in the valley were a dozen stay-behinds from the three companies under Reno's command. Sergeant Charles White, a chunky German immigrant and veteran of the Civil War, was the senior man present. Sergeant White was from M Company. He had taken a Sioux arrow in the arm and, though the wound had been crudely bandaged, it was still painful, to judge from the frequent sighs and groans that he gave forth. He had lost his hat. The other men—mostly from G Company—had been guarding the flanks of the led horses when they were abandoned by the precipitous retreat and they were anything but calm and collected now. But, at Sergeant White's insistent commands, they kept their complaints and speculations below the level of moaning he appeared to have established.

George Herendeen, the young Montana scout, recommended that they release the five or six horses left with them. They did so after stripping the horses. After his contribution with regards to the horses, Herendeen said little. Suddenly, he stood and walked to the clearing and looked across the now deserted prairie. Even Sergeant White was silent as the others watched him study the prairie. Herendeen turned.

"Now's the time," he announced to the demoralized casabiancas. "Don't shoot unless necessary. We don't want to stir up a general engagement. Don't run. Go in skirmish order. Take it cool and we'll get out."

Herendeen started out and the soldiers reluctantly followed him, muttering dolefully. Herendeen turned around, a stern expression on his young-old weather-beaten face.

"I've been in scrapes like this before," he announced in a level voice, "and I know we'll make it if we just keep cool. I can get out alone, I know. If you do what I tell you, I'll get you out too."

Sergeant White spoke up harshly from the rear.

"T'ey vill do vat you vant," he said, "for I vill compel t'em to obey orders. I vill shoot t'e first man who shoots or disobeys orders."

Without another word, the stay-behinds walked out of the timber in a loose line, Herendeen and "Fritz" Sivertsen—a tall Norwegian-born private from M Company—leading the way. Sivertsen had no hat or blouse and his issue gray flannel shirt was a couple of sizes too small.

Sergeant Ferdinand A. Culbertson, a tall, powerfully built young man from A Company, was talking to Lieutenant Varnum.

"C'mon," Varnum commanded briskly as he digested the big noncom's report. The two men half ran to Major Reno.

"Sir," Varnum said perfunctorily, "this man saw Lieutenant Hodgson go down. He saw an Indian trying to scalp Benny and fired at him."

"Go down and try to find him," Reno said at once. "Take as many men as you need."

"Shall we bring him back or bury him?" Varnum asked.

Reno didn't reply at once, his eyes focused far, far away.

"Bury him," he said quietly at last in a broken voice.

Culbertson and Varnum abandoned their mission halfway down the hill.

"We'll wait till Captain Mac brings in the packs," Varnum said. "I know there are some spades on those mules."

The three companies at the north end of the long ridge spread out. For almost five minutes there was a lull. Then the Indians charged.

Sturgis' Gray Horse Troop was caught too far ahead of their led horses and the mounted Indians raced between them shouting, firing, and waving buffalo robes. Four panicked horses were too much for each of the suddenly surrounded horse holders and most of the gray horses bolted away. The frantic horse holders were tangled up in reins while mounted Indians hatcheted and speared them with impunity. The scything mounted charge of the Indians rocketed past the other two companies, expertly cutting out the difficult-to-manage horses and driving them down the slope toward the river.

Tom Custer rode among the swirling horses, firing his self-cocking revolver with cold-blooded effectiveness. But the Indians veered away from the pockets of resistance and concentrated on the horses.

"Cheyenne!" Tom Custer shouted above the whooping din to dark-eyed Lieutenant Harrington. "They're Cheyenne! Every goddam red west of the Missouri is here!"

"The Gray Horse is for it," Harrington replied as the dust

raised by the wild charge and resultant stampede began to lift. He pointed.

The skirmishers of Sturgis' E Company scrambled into a large ditch hastily vacated by the Indians. A few of the stampeded horses had been recaught—a very precious few.

Cooke trotted up on his white horse.

"That's no place for a stand. We should fort up on the high ground," he said.

Tom Custer nodded emphatically.

"Bring them back," he instructed Harrington. "Take everybody from C with you. Hang on to the horses and go slow. Everybody stick together."

Harrington trotted off toward the partially dehorsed C Company. He rapped out the orders and a lonely trumpet began to blow. Tom Custer rode partway down with them until a call from Lieutenant Cooke brought him up short. He galloped toward the top of the knoll.

"George Yates is dead," Cooke told him. "I didn't see it. He was standing one minute and down in the grass the next."

Tom Custer galloped over to handsome Lieutenant van Wyck Reily, who was standing at the rear of a very ragged skirmish line formed by F Company.

"Move down the slope," Tom Custer instructed him. "Keep them off the right flank. Stay together. If they charge again, form square and wait until the rest of us come down to you."

F Company started forward.

Long-haired Boston Custer joined the rescue party, holding General Custer's Remington high for Tom to see. The scar-faced Custer nodded and grinned tightly. Young Autie Reed, pale and serious, followed his youngest uncle.

"Stay together," Tom Custer repeated. "Don't let them ride through you like that again."

"Excuse me, Godfrey," Major Reno told the K Company commander with elaborate politeness, "I am going to have to borrow Mr. Hare from you to act as my adjutant."

Godfrey acquiesced with a curt nod. Hare stood uneasily beside them.

"Lieutenant Hodgson, my adjutant, has been killed," Reno remarked unnecessarily.

Hare's horse had been shot coming up the hill and the three men examined the suffering animal dispassionately. The heavy sorrel had been shot through the jaw and his tongue was lolling grotesquely.

"Take my horse," Godfrey said, without a trace of emotion, to Hare. Reno said nothing as he walked stiffly away from the gruesome sight.

Hare didn't have too far to go down the trail in the direction of the lone tepee to find the packtrain. Captain McDougall was pushing them as fast as he dared while personally riding out front with a drawn pistol. The mules were running—after a fashion—and the troops before and behind them kept them fairly well corralled.

"Major Reno's compliments, sir," Hare reported to Captain Mac. "He'd like a couple of the ammunition packs right away. And the rest of you as soon as you can come."

"Reno?" McDougall asked. "The word I got was that Custer and Reno were split up and that Custer wanted the packs brought straight across to him. Where's Reno?"

Hare gestured behind him.

"Another couple of miles or so," he said. "We haven't heard from Custer, though we heard some shooting from the lower end of the village. We got chased out of the village and lost a lot of men in the process."

McDougall nodded.

"Custer sent an orderly sergeant to me saying it was a big village," the roly-poly packtrain and escort commander said placidly.

"It's the biggest damn village I've ever seen," Hare reported soberly. "And the pony herd—must be twenty thousand of them. I've seen cattle drives, I know."

At McDougall's command, two of the ammunition-bearing mules were cut out of the train and led by mounted troopers to Lieutenant Hare.

"The rest of us'll be along soon," McDougall promised.

Myles Keough was forced to halt a second time. Jim Calhoun's company was deployed and their bay horses suddenly bolted east toward the broken ground behind the ridge. Indians scattered as Keough galloped back along the ridge accompanied by Sergeant Varden and Trumpeter Patton. The three men saw the reason for the stampede at once.

L Company's horse holders looked like porcupines as they lay lifeless on the reverse slope of the hill Calhoun was trying to hold. The big impassive blond brother-in-law of Custer was hatless. He was bent over one-eyed J. J. Crittenden, who crouched awkwardly, an Indian arrow stuck in his back. Crittenden was trying to stand and Calhoun was holding him down. Calhoun looked up as Keough and party jolted to a halt beside him.

"Our ammunition's gone," he said coolly.

Keough turned to Patton.

"Sound Recall," he told the trumpeter as he surveyed his own company under Lieutenant Jim Porter making slow but steady progress north—away from Calhoun.

"Go on," Calhoun told the Irishman calmly. "We'll buy some time for you."

Keough's eyes flashed. "We'll stick together," he said incisively.

Captain Tom Weir of D Company stopped pacing and walked down to where Lieutenant Edgerly and First Sergeant Martin were standing.

"Edgerly," he half whispered, "will you go down with the troop if I go?"

The big handsome second lieutenant studied his superior for a half minute before replying. Weir was scowling with fierce concentration on something and biting his lip.

"Yes, sir," Edgerly said in his deep voice.

Weir glanced over toward Major Reno.

"Well, I will go and get permission from Benteen or Major Reno."

Edgerly nodded and watched his company commander walk up the incline toward Reno.

On the knoll, Lieutenant Cooke led the remaining horses into a tight circle. He stalked around the inside of the stand, shooting horses in the head. His white hat was long gone, his short hair was unruffled, and his long, full Dundrearies twitched as he grimaced before firing the fatal shot each time. The horses pitched to the ground. The cavalrymen inside the macabre "fort" were weeping openly at the sight. The bodies of General George A. Custer, Captain George W. Yates, and Lieutenant Algernon E. Smith were lain neatly inside the circle of dead horses. The soldiers, mostly from F Company, crouched behind the carcasses of the horses and fiddled with their carbines. Cooke, expressionless now, walked the perimeter, relocating badly situated defenders. Sergeant Vickory had planted the regimental banner in the approximate center of the ring and crouched beside it. A little to his left, old Sergeant Hughes crouched beside the planted red-and-blue flag of General Custer.

"Absolutely not," Reno repeated to a flush-faced Captain Weir on the hill. "We are going to stay together as a unit. There are too many of them for three companies—maybe too many for six. We are staying together."

"What are we waiting for?" Weir demanded belligerently, not bothering to soften his speech with token words of respect. Reno flushed angrily, but when he answered, his voice was calm enough.

"We are waiting for the packs," he said simply.

"Didn't you hear those volleys?" Weir demanded, red-faced. "Custer is out there and those volleys were signals for us to guide on. He sent for us. You saw the note. He expects us to ride to the sound of the guns."

"I saw the note," Reno answered in a quavery voice. "I saw the note and I also saw half my men ridden down by the Sioux. We need ammunition. We need medical supplies. We do not need captains telling majors what is expected of them."

"Someone should," Weir raged back, "before Custer is after you with a sharp stick!"

"I didn't hear that, Captain Weir," Reno snapped.

"Like you didn't hear the signal volleys either," Weir muttered as he stalked away. Reno opened his mouth, then closed it as Weir grumbled on. "If we ever get out of this, someone will answer for it, by God!"

Weir reached his own horse in a funny gait and swung into the saddle, quivering with suppressed emotion. He jerked the reins savagely and swung his spurs cruelly into the horse's sides. He cantered forward in the direction of the peaks where Custer had observed Reno in the valley almost two hours before.

Lieutenant Edgerly watched the exchange, but couldn't hear a word. He saw Weir mount and lead out. He watched his company commander for a signal and, seeing none, turned to First Sergeant Martin.

"Well, I guess he got Major Reno's permission, grudging though it may have been."

"Will we be followin' then, sorr?"

"Yes. Mount the command. Forward at a walk."

D Company mounted and, with Lieutenant Edgerly in the lead, followed the trail Custer had left toward the peaks.

Benteen joined Reno.

"I thought we were going to stay together until the packs got up," he remarked, his merry grin still holding up. "Why are you moving out a company of my battalion, if I may ask?"

Reno glared at him.

"Captain Weir was told expressly to remain here until we were situated," he said in a voice thickened by emotion. "He requested permission to move toward the sound of the guns and I emphatically refused him."

"Well," Benteen sighed, "it appears he has gone off on his own hook—in a fit of bravado, no doubt."

"We'll have to order him back," Reno snapped.

Benteen nodded vaguely and, still smiling, made his way toward Captain French.

Reno turned to a trumpeter.

"Sound the Recall," he ordered.

Edgerly heard the trumpet calls and looked back. D Company was in good order behind him. He looked across the broken terrain toward Captain Weir, who was going head-down toward the peaks. Edgerly shrugged.

"Press up, men," he said unnecessarily. "Keep moving."

Tom Custer was riding in the rear of the slow-moving skirmish line formed by the remainder of F Company commanded by young Lieutenant William van Wyck Reily. They fired sporadically and edged their way south along the slope below the knoll. The sky rained arrows and the few horses that were left pitched and bucked frantically. The Indians were firing the arrows in a high arc from concealed positions at the base of the knoll. One arrow landed on Tom Custer's left shoulder with a thunk. He swayed in the saddle and dropped his reins. First Sergeant Michael Kenney, a young Irishman with pale blue eyes, grabbed the trailing reins and gentled the frantic horse. A grizzled private steadied Tom Custer from the other side. The two led the horse and wounded rider back up the slope toward the circle of dead horses.

Lieutenant Reily saw the rearward movement of Sergeant Kenney and halted the F Company skirmish line.

"Back to the top!" he shouted as they hesitated and seemed to waver. The troops needed no urging. They broke for the safety of the high ground out of the range of those deadly arrows.

Lieutenant Harrington saw the movement and halted C Company—or what was left of it—halfway between Sturgis' poorly positioned Gray Horse Troop and the top of the hill. He mounted one of the few horses left in his command and started toward the knoll. His unattended command began to spread out and fall back. Halfway to the top of the knoll, he stopped and stared.

The wounded Tom Custer saw it too. As he was led into the circle and helped to the ground by Sergeant Kenney and Dr. Lord, he jerked his chin to the north and east as Cooke hurried over to him. Cooke turned around.

Outside the circle, Lieutenant Reily saw it—and halted.

For an interminable two minutes, the shocked cavalry officers and men stared at the ridge above and behind the knoll Cooke had fortified so bloodily.

The horizon seemed covered with mounted Indians where none had been only minutes before. They seemed to be waiting and sat immobile on their ponies flank to flank.

"Oh, my God!" Sergeant Kenney breathed in the eerie silence that followed. The Indians in the ravine below had temporarily stopped firing.

"How many of them are there?" Lieutenant Harrington asked aloud. There was no one within fifteen feet to hear or answer.

Tom Custer struggled to his feet, his wounded shoulder held stiffly and the arm below it rigid at his side. With his good hand, he shook off Sergeant Kenney and Dr. Lord. He began to fumble with his pistol, loading it with shaking, bloody fingers and cursing in a listless monotone.

A single Indian detached himself from the solid mass and pranced his pony in front of the others, shouting words that were not heard by the 7th Cavalry companies below him. He was a light-skinned Indian with a single eagle feather. Naked to the waist, he was covered with red zigzag lightning marks and large dots. His black pony was similarly decorated. He was covered with dust—more dust than could possibly have been raised by galloping ponies. It appeared that he had covered himself with dust deliberately. He raised a carbine and dropped it.

The Indians mounted behind him charged.

Lieutenant Reily and what remained of F Company began to run pell-mell for the dubious safety of Cooke's corral. C Company behind Harrington did the same.

Then the Indians below in the ravines and hollows rose up and charged.

Reno was in a towering rage when he spotted Lieutenant Varnum and Sergeant Culbertson.

"I thought it best to wait for some spades off the pack mules," Varnum explained.

"Come on," Reno barked. He led the two men down the steep slope of the hill toward the ill-fated ford. He gathered ten men from A Company on the way down and the party had to trot to keep up with him.

They reached Hodgson's body a few minutes later.

"They took his watch," Varnum announced after a cursory examination. He began to weep. "Those dirty, thieving bastards—"

Reno removed Hodgson's West Point ring and some keys and dropped them into his pocket. He turned and practically ran back up the hill.

"Here come some of ours," Sergeant Culbertson called softly. When Varnum straightened and looked in the direction Culbertson indicated, he saw a party of a dozen troopers crossing the ford on foot. He recognized George Herendeen and some of the men with him.

"Major, the packs are up," Captain McDougall reported.

Reno was staring down at the steep hill toward the ford at the knot of blue uniforms around Varnum's buckskins—all standing over Hodgson's body uncertainly.

"Benny is lying right over there," he said hollowly.

McDougall peered down at the group at the base of the hill. He looked sideways at Reno and, after an awkward pause, turned his attention to the men from A and M Companies fishing rounds of ammunition out of the bags on the mules who had just joined the command on the hill.

He noticed Captain Benteen, hatless, standing beside buck-skinned Tucker French, and began walking slowly toward him.

Reno watched dully as two men from Varnum's burial group returned to the hilltop and snatched two spades from the pack mules after a long argument with the civilian packers. As they started back down the hill, he glanced to his right and saw H and M Companies under Benteen and French mounting up and starting off in the direction Weir had taken.

"Trumpeter," Reno said sternly, "didn't I tell you to sound the Recall?"

"Yes, sir," a bearded soldier replied. "I did and nothing happened."

"I didn't tell you to stop," Reno barked, and turned away to look at the base of the bluff.

Varnum, down below, was shaking hands with the civilian, Herendeen. The soldiers who had accompanied him across the ford were already at the top of the hill and mingling with their companies.

Captain Myles Keough saw the sudden mass move and stopped his own I Company on its way to help out L Company.

"This way!" he called, pointing. I Company turned as one and began to jog forward. The led horses and their holders were unable to keep up. To their right, the east, Indians swarmed up out of the hollows and charged. They drove in between I Company and its led horses and L Company further south along the ridge. The horses were surrounded in an instant by triumphantly whooping Indians who shot and clubbed the horse holders and drove the led horses east toward the badlands.

Keough halted I Company.

"Form a hollow square!" lanky Sergeant Varden shouted above the din.

Keough's mount stumbled and the Irishman howled in pain as an Indian bullet broke his leg and plowed on through into his horse's side.

Trumpeter Patton grabbed his company commander by the nape of the neck and held him half suspended in air until two troopers came to his assistance. It was the last thing he ever did. As he released Keough to the care of the two privates, he pitched forward, a Sioux arrow embedded in his back.

The Indians rode over I Company.

Sergeant John M. Ryan led M Company out behind Benteen's fresh bays. Captain French had remained behind to supervise the stragglers who were just mounting.

Private Fritz Sivertsen, up from the ford with soaked trousers, a gray flannel shirt and no hat, hailed his company commander.

"I'm glad to see you, Fritz," French said with more animation than he had shown all day. "I've got you down on the dead list already."

"Lost my horse, Cap," Sivertsen replied.

French nodded, regaining his customary aloofness. "Grab another" was all he said as he cantered forward to take the lead from Sergeant Ryan and follow Weir and Benteen toward the sound of the guns.

Lieutenant Hare, with an uncertain look in his close-set brown eyes, joined Reno on the hilltop. Reno seemed not to see him and Hare kept glancing at his own company, which, under Godfrey, was moving out with the others. He saw Captain Moylan eyeing him with a questioning look and was about to say something to Reno when the major suddenly ordered: "Get Mr. Herendeen up here!"

Hare started down the slope.

"Not you, Lieutenant," Reno called. "I need you as my adjutant."

Hare rejoined him expectantly. Reno directed a young private from A Company to deliver the summons to Herendeen and beckoned to the Crow Indian scout Half Yellow Face. He turned to Hare.

"I want you to take a message to Captain Weir," he instructed the thin young Texan. "I want you to tell him to report to me as soon as he is successful in reaching General Custer. I want him to tell the general that I have a large number of wounded and that I require assistance. We will be along as soon as we can get ready."

Hare nodded and reached an unclaimed horse in three giant steps. He swung into the saddle and galloped away toward the strung-out companies headed north by west.

Cooke's corral of dead horses wasn't adequate to stem the tide. The Indians leaped their ponies over the obstacles and dashed through the pathetic compound striking out wildly with lance and club. Tom Custer, swaying in the center, was brained by a rider who came up behind him. Lieutenant William W. Cooke was spitted on a lance and died trying frantically to tug it out.

Lieutenant Reily made it inside the dead-horse perimeter only to be pincushioned by arrows. Harrington, still mounted, swerved away from the incoming riders and rode over the ridge headed for the east. The men behind him were cut down in the open. Harrington was pursued by three Indians who fired almost point-blank at his back. He slid off his horse, which kept running east.

The Indians in the west and south gained the lip of the dead-end gully where Lieutenant Jack Sturgis and his E Company were corralled. They stood and fired into the ditch as if shooting diseased cattle.

It was all over in a few minutes.

Myles Keough, coughing handfuls of blood, sat between the bodies of Sergeant Varden and Trumpeter Patton and attempted to raise his pistol at the Indians milling around him. He managed to cock it before a spasm of coughing took him. He dropped the pistol and slumped.

George Herendeen joined Reno a few minutes later.

"What happened?" Reno wanted to know.

"We lost our horses in the timber," the young cowboy reported. "We didn't hear the command to withdraw."

Reno's face darkened as he turned away. He beckoned Half Yellow Face over closer and directed his attention to the lodges of the upper camp. They were being taken down. Reno turned back to the baffled Herendeen.

"Mr. Herendeen, I need your services as an interpreter. I want to know why the lodges are being struck. What are they going to do?"

Herendeen rumbled in Crow, and Half Yellow Face answered with his customary impassiveness.

"They are going away," Herendeen translated.

Reno nodded thoughtfully.

"Mount every man who can ride," Reno instructed Captain Myles Moylan.

"Some of my wounded can't ride, sir," the beetle-browed A Company commander protested.

Reno looked uncertain as Captain McDougall joined them with a raised eyebrow.

"Then you'll have to carry them," he said at last in a weak voice.

Lieutenant Varnum bent over the body of his friend Benny Hodgson and closed the half-opened eye with his own thumb. When he stood, he looked around at the ten-man detail, including the two hovering in the background with spades. He looked down at the body. Except for the gaping hole in his chest and the mangled leg, the likable "Jack of Clubs" might well have been asleep.

"I don't know what to say," Varnum complained to Sergeant Culbertson.

Culbertson turned around and scanned the faces of the burial detail.

"Any of you boys religious?" he asked.

There was a stir, but no answer.

Lieutenant Wallace called down to the burial detail as he led the pitiful remainder of G Company off in the direction the others had gone.

Varnum looked around wildly, but the decision had already been made by the ten enlisted men, who scrambled up the slope devil take the hindmost. Sergeant Culbertson looked at the pinch-faced lieutenant helplessly.

"Where the hell are we running to this time?" Varnum grumbled as he passed the heavyset sergeant on the way back up the hill.

"I don't know, Lieutenant," the noncom puffed behind him, "but I sure ain't going to be left behind again!"

The unburied body of Benny Hodgson lay where the little lieutenant had fallen.

Captain Myles Moylan gazed down at the village as his company was saddling up. The lodge covers of buffalo hide were being replaced and the few poles that had been knocked down were being re-erected.

Buckskinned Charles Varnum joined his erstwhile company commander. Moylan turned to Varnum.

"In my opinion," he said solemnly, "General Custer made the biggest mistake of his career by not taking the whole regiment in on that first attack."

"The last time I heard that kind of statement," Varnum answered, "General Custer was talking about Major Reno and his scout."

"What did he say?"

"He said that the major had made the biggest mistake of his career by not following up the trail and attacking the village."

Moylan gazed thoughtfully at Varnum, but said nothing.

A little to the right of the struggling men and horses of A Company, Major Reno had pulled his horse out of column and gestured for Half Yellow Face and George Herendeen once again.

"How's that?" Reno asked. "The lodges are up again."

Herendeen interpreted Half Yellow Face's solemn reply: "I don't know."

Varnum galloped ahead to Captain McDougall, who was once more shepherding the packs.

"Sir, we need help transporting our wounded. We don't have enough unwounded men to do the job."

McDougall looked back and nodded grimly. With a minimum of words, he dispatched one platoon to help Moylan and Varnum bring up the wounded.

As Captain Weir reached the peaks accompanied by only his orderly, he waved his hat at Lieutenant Edgerly, who was leading D Company up a narrow draw to the east of Weir. Edgerly stared at his company commander, straining his eyes to interpret his hand and arm signals. With a nod of comprehension and a reassuring wave of his own battered black hat, he led D Company up out of the draw onto the high ground to the east of where Weir sat. He dismounted the fifty-man company and formed a skirmish line facing east and north with their backs to the edge of a precipice that dropped into a bowl-like depression.

Benteen's H Company took up positions on the high ground directly across the gorge from Edgerly facing north and west toward the river. Captain French's M Company filled in the head of the rim of the bowl between the other two companies facing north. This left two small gaps between M and the companies on either side of the rim. Godfrey's K Company crammed into the space between French and Benteen; Nick Wallace put his token force from G Company in the other gap, between French and Edgerly.

The companies thus formed an irregular horseshoe along the southern rim of the bowl-like depression that ran north into the badlands between their own positions and the deep coulee Custer had followed to the ford.

Behind them, A and B Companies and the packs were strung out all the way back to the hill Reno had initially retreated to. And their numbers were growing. Privates Brennan and Fitzgerald, both Irish veteran soldiers, joined the packs. They were afoot. The other troopers nodded at them stiffly. Brennan and Fitzgerald were from Tom Custer's C Company. No one asked questions.

"Lost our horses, we did," Brennan said easily by way of explanation.

No one replied.

Sergeant James Flanagan, a large and powerful Irishman who had served in the Army all his adult life, joined Captain Weir as a duty sergeant dispatched from Lieutenant Edgerly. Flanagan, with sharp blue eyes and long brown hair in the Civil War style, had just turned forty.

Weir was straining his eyes to the north where a large cloud of dust was visible about two miles away as the crow flies. On the edges of the dust cloud, mounted Indians could be seen packed densely together. Weir pointed.

"That is Custer over there."

Sergeant Flanagan lowered the field glasses he was looking through and handed them to his company commander.

"Here, Captain," he said respectfully, "you'd better look through these glasses. I think those are Indians."

Through the glasses, Weir could make out Indians riding over the long ridge on the other side of the coulee. The ridge ran almost north-south. The Indians appeared to be firing into the ground. Weir lowered his glasses with a bewildered expression.

Fred Benteen planted H Company's guidon between two large rocks at the top of the highest peak. The forked flag snapped in the breeze—a breeze that was virtually nonexistent in the swales and slopes below. Benteen rode down the reverse slope of the high ground and joined Captain Weir as the latter was hearing Major Reno's compliments from Lieutenant Hare as well as instructions to open communications with Custer. Weir caught Benteen's eye and gestured at the dust cloud in the distance.

"Custer is giving it to them over there," Weir said. "We'll have to swing wide to the east and follow his trail."

"We're strung out all the way back to the first hill," Benteen answered. "This makes no sense. If we're not careful, Mr. Lo will stampede us like he did Reno in the bottom. And the way we're strung out, he could gobble us up one company at a time."

"Moylan's having trouble transporting the wounded," Ed Godfrey announced as he trotted up to join the conference.

"What's this?" Weir asked sharply. "Are they coming this way?"

Sergeant Flanagan had his glasses up in a flash.

"Indians, sir," he said grimly, "headed straight for us. Hundreds of 'em."

The four officers scanned the ground between them and the advancing Indians and the dust cloud as well as their own troop dispositions.

"This is a hell of a place to fight Indians," Benteen concluded gruffly. "I am going to see Reno and propose that we go back to where we lay before starting out."

While the officers conferred, the enlisted men watched the horizon anxiously. Several of Benteen's men swore they had spotted two dismounted troopers making their way toward the command on foot over the badlands. Sergeant McCurry, the burly first sergeant, pooh-poohed the report. But he was unable to deny the existence of the smiling half-breed who rode into H Company's lines a few minutes later. His horse was staggering and his long black hair was held up by a white handkerchief.

"Why, it's Billy Cross!" one of the older veterans remarked.

Billy Cross grinned. "Horse gave out," he grunted. "Couldn't keep up."

"Where's Custer?" one of his audience demanded.

Cross shrugged.

The troopers around him melted away with distant looks on their faces.

"I was going to suggest the same thing myself," Reno told them when he heard Benteen's proposal. "This march was unnecessary. I said so from the start, but no one listens to me any more."

Weir flushed and moved his horse away, his crooked nose in the air. He borrowed Sergeant Flanagan's glasses again and studied the Indian advance out of earshot of the conference. Ed Godfrey had remained behind when the others sought out Reno and he looked from the distant conference to the skyline with an uneasy frown.

"In my opinion," Benteen told Reno, "Custer has struck the

north end of the village about where the dust cloud is and either has been rebuffed or has ridden through them. In either case, I'm afraid he has abandoned us to our fate, while he rides north for Terry and the Yellowstone."

"So what do we do?" Reno asked.

"Fort up on the first defensible piece of ground we come to and wait for Custer—or Terry."

"Or Crook," Hare contributed. "Crook's on his way north from Fort Laramie."

Reno stared into the large blue eyes of Fred Benteen. At length, he dropped his gaze.

"We should stick together," he muttered.

And, with that, he wheeled his horse and headed toward the rear of the column, where McDougall and Moylan were struggling with the mules and wounded.

Captain Benteen rode off toward his own company on the high ground.

Lieutenant Hare looked confused.

H Company was the first of the companies on the rim of the bowl to retire. They mounted and walked slowly south in good order. French, in the middle, saw the move and immediately moved his command.

Lieutenant Ed Godfrey watched the maneuvers of the two companies to either side of him with a scowl of perplexity on his normally expressionless aquiline face. Hare rode up to him.

"The order has been given to pull back to the first position," Hare said uncertainly as he watched, with Godfrey, the precipitous withdrawal of Captain French.

The M Company veterans of the valley fight needed no urging to get out of the way of the oncoming Sioux. What began as a walk accelerated without commands to a very rapid trot. Lieutenant Wallace, on the other side of French's command, shouted a warning to Lieutenant Edgerly, who was scanning the south side of the bowl for a sign of Captain Weir while keeping an eye cocked on the advancing Indians.

Edgerly ordered that the led horses be brought to the skirmish line and, this being done, D Company "stood to horse" while the Indians swarmed in from the low ground to the east and up the bowl from the north. Horses began to buck and dance as long-range shots began to fall on D Company.

"Who gave the order?" Godfrey asked as he watched the exposed D Company come under long-range fire.

"Major Reno," Hare said promptly.

"Someone ought to tell young Edgerly," Godfrey remarked, as if he were discussing the weather. "He's out on a limb and I don't see Weir anywhere."

Hare galloped down the draw, passing Captain Weir, and up the far side into D Company's position.

"Where's Major Reno?" Edgerly demanded above the din of bullets zipping in. Hare was still mounted and had to stoop—but only a little—to be heard by Edgerly, who was standing calmly alone on the highest point of the east ridge.

"Gone back to look after the mules," Hare answered.

Edgerly shook his head and a sardonic smile crossed his handsome face momentarily.

"For Christ's sake, Lieutenant!" one of the long-suffering D Company privates burst out at last.

Edgerly grinned broadly.

"All right, men," he boomed, "out we get!"

"Do you want me to cover D Company?" owlish Frank Gibson asked his boss, Captain Benteen. "Edgerly's pretty exposed—"

"I don't think we'll be attacked now," Benteen answered. "The Indians are too far away and besides, it will be dark soon. I think we should concentrate on getting back together again without leaving anyone behind like they did in the bottom."

"Shouldn't we sound the Recall?"

Benteen stopped and turned around. Gibson circled him expectantly.

"I see Edgerly is moving now," Benteen said. "Captain Weir must have command again."

Captain Weir was indeed once more in command of D Company. He slowed the leading riders down as he encountered them in the draw and formed a column of fours of the lead platoon. He led south at a rapid trot.

On the high ground, big Win Edgerly was having trouble mounting his horse. The horse, spooked by the whoops of the Indians who were nearly on top of them and the whine of the bullets that had been raining on them for some minutes, kept turning and shying away as the handsome young giant tried to mount him. Edgerly threw his black hat in disgust and didn't bother to retrieve it.

Vincent Charlie, a tall red-headed Swiss immigrant who served as a farrier in D Company, fell off his own horse with a shriek of pain. Edgerly was beside him in two bounds. The farrier had been shot in the hip and had hit his head in falling.

"For Gott's sake, don't leave me, Lieutenant," he pleaded as he saw the Indians moving in.

"Get down in the draw," Edgerly told him. "Stay low. I'll bring a skirmish line back for you."

Vincent Charlie nodded gratefully, his face torn between terror and trust.

Edgerly sprang to his horse and tried once again to mount. The horse shied away. Finally, Edgerly's orderly, Private Charles Sanders, swung his own horse on the opposite side of the recalcitrant horse and Edgerly was able to mount in one fluid motion. Sanders, a tall dark German immigrant, was laughing.

The two galloped down into the draw just south of the rim of the bowl where Weir had reassumed command minutes earlier. They had to race to catch the rapidly retreating D Company.

"What did you see to laugh about?" Edgerly asked Sanders.

"I vas laughing to see vat poor shots t'ose Indians vere," Sanders shouted above the clatter their galloping horses made over the barren stony soil of the draw. "T'ey vas shooting too low and t'eir bullets vas spattering dust like drops of rain."

Edgerly favored his smiling striker with a hurried glance of amazement and approval.

"I left a wounded man back there," Edgerly told Weir, as the latter rode head-down due south. Edgerly raised his deep voice. "I told him I'd be back with a skirmish line."

"I'm sorry," Weir said, without looking at the younger man, "orders are to fall back on the first hill."

"I promised him!" Edgerly cried in dismay and disbelief.

Weir looked at the big man galloping beside him for the first time. His face was flushed and his small eyes were hard.

"I can't help it," he snapped. "The orders are positive. We must go back."

"Request permission to go back alone," Edgerly said stiffly.

"Request denied, Mr. Edgerly. Carry on."

French's M Company and Weir's D Company thundered on. Benteen turned in his saddle and stared at the rapid retreat.

"This won't do," he told his lieutenant, Frank Gibson. "Take the troop ahead to where Major Reno is and place them in a perimeter. I will join you shortly."

Gibson nodded grimly and rode to the head of fast-trotting H Company to put some order into the withdrawal.

Benteen beckoned Captain Tucker French of M Company and paced his long-legged bay in short half circles waiting for the square-faced little commander of M Company to join him beside the trail. Benteen described a line from one end of the draw to the other with his hand.

"Put your troop there," Benteen told French. "Close the back door."

French nodded jerkily and cantered back toward his retreating command.

Private Jimmy Wynn of D Company lost control of his horse. Wynn, a gray-haired tailor who was very fat and red-faced, struggled ineptly to slow down the stampeding horse. He leaned as far backward as his back would allow and rode face to the sky—all the way to Reno's Hill.

"Whoa," he kept bawling. "Whoa."

Private Wynn—or rather, his horse—outdistanced all the other four companies and did not stop until he reached the selected position. The troops he passed stared in amazement and then began to laugh at the ludicrous sight of the fat old man being led by his horse. Wynn's boots came out of the stirrups and his short fat legs bounced up and down in time with the horse's hooves.

Even Lieutenant Edgerly couldn't help smiling. The troops were all laughing, almost hysterically.

Eagle-beaked Ed Godfrey of K Company wasn't laughing. He was looking over his shoulder at the steadily advancing (and increasing) Indians. He watched impassively as French's rear guard thundered past. Weir's D Company was the last in line, but badly strung out. Weir didn't look to either the right or the left as he led his command past Godfrey's.

Godfrey looked up and down the draw and saw Indians massing in D Company's rear. He looked over and caught sight of Captain Benteen gesturing imperiously.

"Look here!" Godfrey shouted to Hare, who was riding beside him. "Hell's to pay!"

The two West Pointers dismounted every third man in K Company and formed a small skirmish line facing north, protecting the rear of the retreating troops. Benteen waved approval.

"Fire!" Hare screamed.

White smoke belched from the guns of at least fifteen carbines. "Fire!" the thin Texan repeated, as Godfrey watched from horseback a few yards south of the line. Another group was dismounted and a third, leaving the Number Fours with three horses—which they led very slowly and in good order into the perimeter being established by hatless, white-haired Fred Benteen, who seemed to be everywhere.

The Indians charged in from the east and Benteen placed Moylan's A Company in front of a finger-shaped ridge to block their advance. He ordered Tom Weir's D Company—which had just come in—to take up a position behind a longer ridge running northwest to southeast so as to protect Moylan's left flank. Moylan didn't have enough men to stretch his line far enough to make contact with Weir's well-chosen position. Benteen spotted the narrow gap and beckoned to Lieutenant Wallace of G Company. He pointed at the hole.

"Wallace," he said calmly, "put your troop right here."

"I have no troop," Wallace replied aggrievedly, "only three men."

"Well, stay there with your three men and don't let them get away," Benteen said almost jocularly. In a low, confidential tone, he added; "I will have you looked out for."

One of the ammunition mules stampeded and ran out in front of Captain Moylan's line. The troops shouted almost hysterically, but the mule only kept running. The Indians had dismounted and were moving forward on foot, taking cover behind every clump of sagebrush and moving closer to Moylan's line and the stampeded mule.

Sergeant Richard P. Hanley of Tom Custer's C Company had been left in charge of the mules for that company. The tall, black-haired Civil War veteran thought he recognized the mule as Barnum, one that C Company's detail was responsible for. Hanley yelled at Private McGuire, the florid-faced young trooper who had talked to Mitch Bouyer only the night before. McGuire was holding a horse. Hanley mounted the horse and galloped out between the line and the advancing Indians. Lieutenant Varnum yelled at him to stop, but he kept going, driving his horse between the mule and the Indians, who began firing at him. Bullets whizzed around him and plucked at his rolled-up sleeves, but he kept his head down and forced the panicked mule to turn in toward the lines. He ignored the now heavy fire and reached for the mule's bridle.

"Sergeant," Myles Moylan called out sternly, "come back in before you are killed!"

"Give up," the watching soldiers urged.

But grimly, Hanley kept after the mule. He lunged forward again and again, reaching for the bridle, only to miss. The mule, to avoid his new tormenter, began to trot away toward the cavalry lines and a waiting Private McGuire. Sergeant Hanley never managed to even touch the elusive mule, but his herding tactics paid off a few minutes later when McGuire seized the trailing bridle and pulled the mule to safety behind the ridge where Lieutenant Gus Mathey was corralling and picketing the stray animals. Sergeant Hanley returned to his post behind the lines. Moylan's men cheered wildly for a minute or two and then settled down to the grim business of fighting off the advancing Indians.

McGuire was astonished to find Private Peter Thompson of C Company with the packs as he led Barnum back.

"Thompson, where the devil have you been?" he demanded.

"Watson and I dropped out," the stocky red-headed Scotsman

said. "He was kicking his horse to get it going again and it bolted. I lost mine trying to help him. We've been walking all afternoon. We saw the guidon on the peak and started for it, but everyone was running away. We yelled but nobody heard us."

"Your horse is gone?" McGuire repeated incredulously. He shook his head as Thompson nodded wearily.

"Why, I saw it just a minute ago," McGuire said.

"Where?"

McGuire led him to the lathered horse. Thompson eyed the horse fondly and began removing the saddle, running his hands over the sweating flanks of the horse reassuringly. Just then, the horse staggered and a fine mist of red drenched the two C Company men. The horse fell heavily—shot through the head. McGuire leaped back and began to move away. Thompson, freckled with blood, was still petting the stricken horse. McGuire turned away with a shudder.

Major Reno was behind Weir's company when Godfrey at last came into the perimeter with the tail of K Company. Benteen put Godfrey's troops to the left of Weir behind the ridge that commanded a view of the draw down which the entire command had sallied forth and then retreated.

"Look here, Benteen," Reno called, "you look out for that side and I'll look after the lines over here."

He gestured vaguely to the south, where Benteen had already established French's M Company, then McDougall's B Company, and finally, on the most exposed slope to the south, his own H Company. Benteen nodded and dismounted. He gave his horse to a private securing horses in the rear and began to walk the line Reno had designated. He said nothing to French, as the latter was absorbed in shooting at Indians who had reappeared at the ford where Reno had recrossed the Little Big Horn in such a hurry. The Indians had now surrounded the seven companies and were working their way up the slopes. Benteen shifted a few of French's troops who were badly situated and moved on.

Roly-poly Captain Mac hailed him. They quickly agreed on the position for B Company and coordinated their respective flank positions. Benteen was about to walk on when McDougall plucked at his sleeve and lowered his voice confidentially.

"Fred, I think you'd better take charge and run the thing," he said. "Our esteemed major doesn't know which end he is standing on to all appearances. He's done nothing that I can see to prepare the command for a defense. If we're not careful, we'll have another Fort Phil Kearny massacre on our hands. You'd better see to things and give the necessary orders."

Benteen nodded and winked. He squeezed the arm of the B Company commander and walked on without another word. Lieutenant Charles Varnum joined him.

"Need an adjutant?" he asked.

Benteen nodded, saying nothing but maintaining his infectious grin. The two men headed toward Lieutenant Gibson and the much-strung-out H Company.

Across the perimeter from Benteen, Lieutenant Hare had rejoined Lieutenant Godfrey.

"Adjutant or no adjutant, I'm staying with you," he declared to his long-nosed commander.

Godfrey raised an eyebrow.

"Reno doesn't need an adjutant," Hare elaborated.

Godfrey only smiled and clapped his young lieutenant on the shoulder. The two began to make the rounds up and down K Company's position.

M and B Companies were in excellent positions—their backs covered by high ground occupied by the other companies and their front well selected for defense. H Company was exposed on slightly higher ground to their left and took the brunt of the Indian fire on the western side of the perimeter.

The other three companies were well situated except for Godfrey's left flank. Godfrey moved his troops to better positions and placed his able first sergeant, DeWitt Winney, in a position to monitor potential trouble. The heaviest fire was directed at A Company under Myles Moylan, who had fortuitously dragged large pack saddles and wooden boxes into his lines to use as barricades. The troops dug pits for themselves with every utensil they could get their hands on, from the picks and spades lifted from the packs to knives, cups, and even spoons.

In spite of the heaviest and most accurate fire, Moylan had only one casualty, a young Scottish private named Moodie, who was hit by a bullet that had passed through two boxes. It might not have been fatal had it not entered his eye.

D Company had two men wounded. B Company had two men wounded also. D Company's casualties were leg wounds; B Company's were neck wounds and both the victims refused to leave the line. They were Sergeant Benjamin C. Criswell, a short, dark West Virginian who had a younger brother in the ranks, and fair-haired Private Charles Cunningham, an older soldier from New York. Both men had their wounds dressed in the lines and refused to leave for the safety of the "hospital" Dr. Porter had erected in the center of the corralled pack mules.

Just before dusk, First Sergeant DeWitt Winney of K Company raised up and yelled. When the nearest man reached him, Winney was dead, a Sioux bullet through the head.

A few feet away, Trumpeter Julius Helmer was shot through the bowels. He was gently carried across the compound and deposited at the mat of blankets behind B Company that Dr. Porter had designated a hospital. He screamed every step of the way, holding his lower abdomen and writhing in agony. He died a few minutes after Dr. Porter had examined him and dolefully shook his head.

Corporal Callahan, a young man from Boston, died with a Sioux arrow through his neck. He was the first victim of the newest Indian tactic. They had begun plunging fire with their arrows, and when the troopers shifted position to dodge the wooden shafts, Indian marksmen tried to pick them off.

H Company, under Benteen, was the most exposed. By nearly dark, it was a shambles. First Sergeant Joseph McCurry was the youngest first sergeant in the regiment, perhaps in the Army. He was a professional class baseball pitcher, the pride (and captain) of the company's baseball team known as the Benteen Baseball Club. He also had organized other sports in the company as well as the glee club. McCurry reported tonelessly to Benteen.

"Pahl's bad hurt. Right shoulder and back. Bullet and arrow. No one saw it happen. Both the Bishops have been hit in the arms. Same for Black, Cooper, and Farley. Moller got a thigh wound. Damned arrow again. I don't know how it found him. Phillips and Severs are the serious cases."

Benteen grunted and nodded. "Looks like we lost a third base-man and a right fielder for sure. Maybe a shortstop too. Careful, son, let's not lose our ace pitcher." He clapped the young man affectionately on the shoulder.

"Oh, yes," McCurry added with a fractional smile, "the German kid, Windolph, got shot in the butt. He's okay."

Benteen grinned, nodded, and started to walk away. "Sir," McCurry called after him, "you reckon they'll be gone in the morning?"

Benteen stopped, turned around, and walked back close to his husky young first sergeant. His voice was low, a mere whisper.

"I don't think so," was all he said.

Night—
Sunday, June 25, 1876

The lower the sun went down, the fewer and further between were the shots and flights of plunging arrows. By 9 P.M. shooting had stopped almost entirely and the officers began to circulate without bending over or running. The sky had become increasingly obscured as time wore on due to the large amounts of discharged black powder with its concomitant white smoke.

Now it began to sprinkle.

Snowy-headed Fred Benteen walked the perimeter posting sentinels and kicking them awake. Part of the way he was accompanied by Lieutenant Gibson, but when he left the H Company front, he was accompanied by the impetuous Lieutenant Varnum, who was every bit as sleepy as Benteen himself. In front of M Company, Varnum collapsed. Private Anton Siebelder picked him up like a baby and carried him to a safe spot near the "hospital" and rolled him up in a blanket.

Captain Thomas Weir sought out Lieutenant Ed Godfrey, who was giving Lieutenant Hare some instructions about a picket line. When the tall Texan disappeared, Weir stepped forward with an apologetic cough and an embarrassed smile.

"I want to thank you, Godfrey, for saving my troop," he said sincerely. He seemed to want to say more and, unable to hold the unblinking stare of the younger man, toed the sandy soil with his boot aimlessly.

"Goddy," he said quietly at last, "if there should be a conflict of judgment between Reno and Benteen as to what we should do, whose orders would you obey?"

"Benteen's," Godfrey replied quickly and matter-of-factly.

Weir nodded with a pleased smile and, after a moment's hesitation, made his way in the direction of French's and McDougall's commands purposefully.

Godfrey watched him go without expression.

In the timber that Reno had so precipitously abandoned, Lieutenant DeRudio and the civilian, Fred Gerard, were having trouble with the two horses that were left between the four men. Gerard's began to whinny and stamp the ground. The four men peered anxiously through the brush to see if any of the noise was attracting the Indians who were still wandering around.

The half-breed, Jackson, jumped up and grabbed a handful of grass. He stuffed it into the mouth of Gerard's horse and tied it fast. He then tied the two horses' heads together and patted them both reassuringly. He leered at Gerard.

"What ees eet?" DeRudio demanded peevishly of Gerard.

"Mine's a stallion," the black-eyed interpreter answered briefly. "Billy's here is a mare."

"They sure picked a hell of a time to get frisky," O'Neill commented.

Myles Moylan was having difficulty finding an NCO to command his picket line. The Indians were not to be seen, but could be heard racing their ponies up and down the draw to Moylan's left—no doubt messengers between the chiefs on the east of the cavalry position and the ones back down in the village.

Moylan didn't want Burke to go, in case Culbertson, his acting first sergeant, was hit. Sergeant Fehler, a middle-aged German, was next in line in terms of seniority, but he refused point-blank. Young Sergeant Easley pleaded duty the previous night. Finally, Sergeant Stanislas Roy, the dark little Frenchman, volunteered.

"Send six men," Moylan advised the doughty Roy, "all volunteers. Sit them out there in groups of two. Don't let anyone go to sleep. Keep one of the pair talking at all times. If the Indians move in, shoot and run. You are our warning—our eyes and ears in the dark."

"I don't think the Indians will do anything more until daylight," Roy said stolidly.

"Privately," Moylan replied, "I don't either, but some of us are going to have to sleep tonight and I don't want anyone's throat being cut by an Indian because I wasn't vigilant."

Roy nodded solemnly and rounded up six "volunteers." One of them refused at the last minute. Roy took his place without a word and withered the pull-out with a scornful look. Two Irish bunkies named Gilbert and McClurg were the first to be posted. Both were young men. Roy picked an older Irishman for his own partner in the lonely, dangerous picket line. The older man was thirty-five-year-old, gray-haired, florid-faced Andrew Connor, as good a man with a gun as with a bottle. A fair-haired New Yorker named Neil Bancroft and a sturdy Indiana farm boy named David Harris completed the contingent.

The six men sat in three equally spaced groups of two about fifty yards in front of Moylan's line, talking quietly among themselves and listening for Indians.

Private John (Old Neutriment) Burkman, Custer's striker, who had been left with Dandy, the general's second mount, in the packtrain, stalked away from the two men seated cross-legged on the single blanket behind Moylan's position. Burkman's face was a thundercloud.

"Well, I wonder where the Murat of the American cavalry is tonight," Reno was saying with a sardonic smile to a very tired Captain Benteen, as the two men sat on an Army blanket on the little knoll.

"He's watering his horses in the Yellowstone by now," Benteen replied. "Sleeping like a babe. He went off and left a part of his command once before at the Washita and I believe he has done it again."

"What do we do now?"

Benteen heaved his massive shoulders in an indifferent shrug. "Hold this position until relieved."

"I think we should try to get a message through to Terry up north," the dark-faced major said. "We have some Indian scouts with us still by some miracle and they should be able to get through."

Benteen nodded wearily.

"Benteen," Reno whispered, "I have been thinking it over and

I have decided to do something, to try something, that is. We cannot just sit here. Tomorrow the reds will be all over us."

Benteen nodded without comment.

"Mount every man who can ride," Reno proposed confidentially. "Destroy such property as cannot be carried, abandon our position, and make a forced march back to our supply camp."

"What about the wounded who can't ride?" Benteen rumbled.

"Oh, we'll have to abandon those who cannot ride."

The darkness hid Benteen's reaction, but the flash of white that was his ever-present grin vanished. When he spoke finally, his voice was low and thick with feeling.

"No, Reno," he said. "You can't do that."

In the valley, DeRudio, Fred Gerard, and their two companions discussed escape.

"We strip the horses, see?" Gerard whispered hoarsely. "Everything but the blankets. We carry the guns and ammunition and leave the rest. We mount two to a horse and take off across the prairie toward the place where we forded this afternoon."

DeRudio shook his head emphatically.

"We must sneak across," he insisted. "Eef they hear us, they weel come to look for us, and when they find us, they weel shoot."

"We shoot back," Jackson the half-breed grunted.

"There are more of them than us," DeRudio argued.

Gerard nodded slowly.

"You're right. Besides, I don't think we could outrun them mounted double."

Gerard and Jackson mounted after gingerly disengaging the tied horses. DeRudio and the G Company man, O'Neill, held on to the tails and the two-horse, four-man party started out.

Halfway across the flats, they walked into a small group of painted Sioux holding horses.

"Haugh!" one of them called and began to jabber in Lakota.

Gerard spurred his horse to the left toward the river and Jackson followed suit. DeRudio and O'Neill were carried right through the middle of the astonished Indians. They clung desperately to the flying horses. The rough ground just short of the river embankment proved their undoing. They tumbled.

DeRudio was fastidiously brushing his tunic when O'Neill

grabbed him roughly by the collar and pushed him into a run toward the river. To their right, another group of Indians shouted and began to shoot. The two men afoot plunged into the Little Big Horn River.

In the middle of the river, Gerard's stallion tired of his swim and attempted to mount Jackson's mare. The resulting entanglement spilled the riders and the current carried them away from the struggling horses.

Meanwhile, DeRudio and O'Neill found themselves on a small island in the middle of the river. They hurried to the east bank and ran smack into another party of Indian pickets. The two startled cavalrymen plunged into the thick underbrush in the center of the island. The Indians fled.

On the opposite bank, Jackson and Gerard took stock. They had the clothes they wore and one knife, Gerard's.

"This is it," he informed Jackson, showing him the knife.

The two men worked their way north without another word exchanged. They moved as swiftly and silently as they could in their waterlogged clothes—away from the river—and Indians.

DeRudio and O'Neill were separated. O'Neill clung tightly to his Springfield and whirled as a branch cracked behind him. Even in the faint moonlight, he could make out the white hair of Lieutenant DeRudio. DeRudio had his pistol drawn.

"O'Neill?" he whispered loudly, querulously. He sighed as he recognized the G Company man at last. "They are all gone," he announced.

The two men began to strip off their waterlogged clothes and place them over some convenient branches to dry.

Benteen found two ammunition mules behind H Company untended and headed for the river below. He corralled them with the help of a half dozen privates from his own company and led them back to the picket Lieutenant Mathey had established.

He tapped the dottle from his black briar pipe on the heel of his boot and sucked noisily on the now empty pipe as Lieutenant Gus Mathey reported in response to Benteen's loud summons.

"Bible Thumper," he told the profane Frenchman, "you have more men down here than any of us have on the line. Can't you keep track of a few Army mules?"

Mathey opened his mouth to protest, but Benteen suddenly began to shout in a rare burst of anger.

"Are you only good for doing Custer's dirty work? There are— or there were—only twenty-four ammo mules. If you can do nothing else competently, for your own sake, keep those few in hand. Never mind running to GAC, he isn't here. I'm here. And if I find another one of those goddamned mules running away from you, I am going to plant my boot right square up the middle of your butt!"

"I am doing the best I can," Mathey answered stiffly.

"Your *best?* Well, Bible Thumper, apparently your best isn't up to it. It's not good enough for me. I would *suggest*"—he accentuated the word sarcastically—"I would suggest that if you want to sit easy for the rest of your days, that you add a dose of real effort to your best. Beginning right now. I mean it, by God!"

He pivoted and strode off, leaving Mathey white-faced and speechless.

"What are you doing here?" Reno demanded of two civilian packers, Churchill and Frett.

"We are looking for something to eat," one of them answered the dark-faced major, who had accosted them among the packs.

"And some ammunition," the other added hastily.

"Are the packs tight?" Reno asked sarcastically.

"What do you mean tight?" Frett asked warily, after an exchange of glances with his partner.

Reno cuffed him hard.

"I mean tight, goddam you, tight," he said in an indistinct voice. He tossed his head back as he swallowed from a large quart container. It splattered Churchill as the major lowered it clumsily. It was brandy.

Reno suddenly produced a carbine, which he leveled at the two civilians.

"If I catch you skulking around here again," he threatened, "I will kill you!"

The two packers vanished.

Lieutenant Varnum, up from a much-needed nap where Siebelder had laid him, wandered over to A Company.

"Major Reno told me to get a message out," Varnum informed Sergeant Burke. "Do you want to go out with it?"

"Well, leftenant," the Irishman replied, "Captain Moylan wants me for duty sergeant as Culbertson is first sergeant now. Besides, you'll not find me volunteerin' for nothin'."

Burke searched the pinched features of the young lieutenant with a tight smile on his own broad face.

"But I will go if ordered," he added quietly.

Varnum nodded and walked off in the direction of Reno's blankets.

"I don't see how you can sleep," Reno told Lieutenant Edgerly peevishly.

Edgerly didn't answer, but returned to his own company with the major's blessing for a proposed move that would fill in a gap between D Company and the minuscule force under Lieutenant Wallace that was G Company.

Varnum handed a note to Reno and the older man strained to read it by the light of a flickering match.

"What is this about ponies?" he demanded.

"The scouts want General Terry to know they captured some ponies," Varnum replied.

"I care nothing for a bunch of ponies," Reno snapped. "Who authorized you to add this to my message?"

"Major," Varnum almost shouted, "you are asking these men to go in jeopardy of their lives to deliver a message containing a lot of apologies and self-justification from you! They figure they have a right to have their own deeds reported."

"Mr. Varnum," Reno said in a shaky, quiet voice, "your insolence and insubordination are intolerable. You will have that message—that original message—delivered as ordered. And you will refrain from adding your own ideas either on paper or verbally to me or anyone else. Do you understand?"

"I understand perfectly," Varnum snapped back. As he stalked away, he tore the message to shreds.

It was a restless night for the seven companies of the 7th Cavalry trapped on the hill. The wounded moaned piteously and Dr. Porter dispensed the dwindling water carefully.

"We need more water," he told Lieutenant Ed Godfrey.
Godfrey nodded thoughtfully.

Benteen didn't sleep for the third night in a row. He made the
rounds with Gibson and instructed the men on the extreme left
flank of H Company to dig a trench. They used the only tools
they could find—a pick and several knives—and succeeded only in
constructing a low spot protected by two mounds of earth. It was
so small it could provide protection only if the occupants lay
prone. The rest of the company was forced to make do with packs
and boxes which Benteen borrowed from the packtrains with increasing frequency.

The hours of darkness passed all too quickly, without any incident. The Indians raced ponies in the ravines, masked by darkness
and distance. And across the river, they continued to send up a
hellish racket that seemed to consist of chants and drums. The
men hadn't eaten since daylight of the previous day. One man in
M Company tried to eat a hardtack cracker, but his mouth was so
dry he couldn't swallow and had to spit it out like so much flour.
There were cans of fruit in the packs, but Major Reno would not
allow them to be opened for the juice alone.

Monday, June 26, 1876

At dawn, Benteen ordered Trumpeter Martin, Custer's last messenger, to blow Reveille and, walking the perimeter, passed on the same instructions to each company trumpeter.

"I want the reds to know there is still a fighting force on this hill," he said, "as well as our own people—stragglers and whatnot."

Benteen continued his circuit of the seven-company position. A single sniper fired at him as he hunkered down on the reverse slope of his own company's position to catch a few winks. The bullet struck the heel of his boot with such force that it partially came off. Benteen pulled it all the way off, absently murmuring, "Pretty close call."

Trumpeter Martin saw the stocky senior captain toss the shredded heel contemptuously in the direction of the Indian sniper.

"Try again!" Benteen shouted to the early-morning light with a grim laugh.

On the island where they had spent the rest of the night, Lieutenant Carlo DeRudio and Private O'Neill heard the trumpets as they were donning their uniforms, which had dried after a fashion on the branches of a nearby tree. DeRudio spotted a figure in buckskin wearing a low white hat and riding a stockinged sorrel. The figure was opposite the island, downriver, at the head of a small party of nondescript Indians.

"That's Tom Custer and the scouts he always has weeth heem," he informed O'Neill.

"Tom!" DeRudio shouted, running toward the group, "Tom Custer! Send your horse across here!"

The figure stopped momentarily and then the whole group moved toward the riverbank. DeRudio stepped out into the open, waving his arms and smiling broadly. The group on the other side of the river seemed to hesitate.

"Here I am!" the little Italian shrilled. "Don't you see me?"

O'Neill rushed forward and pulled the excited lieutenant away. "Damned if those aren't Indians," he growled.

DeRudio was about to protest when "Tom Custer" and the "scouts" opened fire. Waving a Winchester 1866 "brass boy" carbine, their leader plunged into the river toward the island. The rest fired from the banks at the underbrush where DeRudio and O'Neill had dived.

"Tom Custer, eh?" O'Neill demanded as they paused, winded, before a mass of tangled tree roots at the opposite end of the island from their pursuers.

"Eet was hees horse. I would know eet anywhere," DeRudio insisted.

They crawled under cover and divided up the ammunition. There were twenty-five carbine rounds and twelve revolver rounds, including the six DeRudio had in his gun. They shook hands solemnly.

"You're the best shot, Lieutenant," O'Neill said simply. "Just save the last for me. Don't let them take me alive."

DeRudio nodded gravely.

Private Richard B. Dorn of B Company walked over to where Captain McDougall lay and gently shook him awake. He stepped back as his company commander stirred and listened to the fusillade of fire from the valley below. McDougall rolled groggily to his knees. Dorn's head virtually exploded.

The fight was on.

Sergeant Roy and his picket line scampered back.

Showers of arrows arched from hidden gullies and draws all around the cavalry positions. Carbines began to pop with the telltale puffs of black powder giving away their positions. The soldiers returned the fire with greater accuracy and less panic than the day before. Benteen walked calmly upright behind the lines, puffing his bow pipe, encouraging individuals and directing fire all around the perimeter.

Private Thomas E. Meador of H Company was in the process

of removing an overcoat he had donned for the night when a bullet from behind H Company's exposed left flank struck him in the chest. Private Charles Windolph, a small dark German immigrant, watched in horror from his relatively safe position prone behind the mounds. Windolph had been nicked in the buttocks the night before and was unable to sit properly anyway. He aimed at the Indian who had shot Meador and fired. He missed.

Frank Mann, a civilian packer who had attached himself to Moylan's A Company, had been firing from behind a breastwork of hardtack boxes. The men nearest him noticed a sudden silence from his position and one of the bravest of the lot crawled over to investigate. He touched Mann exploratively and the civilian's head lolled lifelessly. He had been shot through the temple.

Sergeant Roy, the tough little Frenchman who had commanded the picket line during the night, covered Mann with a blanket and took up the position the packer had been holding. He was bleary-eyed from lack of sleep, but he banged away with authority. Reloading, Roy checked the positions of the five men who had been up all night with him and saw they were all up and firing. He smiled grimly and punched off another round.

H Company caught the worst of it again. Trumpeter Ramell and First Sergeant McCurry were slightly wounded. Lieutenant Frank Gibson stayed as low as he could get to the ground. As long as the 7th Cavalrymen stayed down, they were relatively safe from enemy fire. But ammunition supplies ran low and it became necessary to make frequent trips through exposed terrain to the pack mules to replenish. Every trip added another wounded man to the list McCurry was grimly keeping.

"Connelly, McLaughlin," he reported to an inquiring Benteen, who seemed to lead a charmed life exposed to the galling fire. "Voit, Bishley, and Hughes," he recited.

Benteen nodded glumly, relighting his pipe.

"Sir," McCurry said earnestly, "if we keep dragging men off the line to the hospital like this, we won't have a line left. We're already spread damn thin."

"Those fellas on the other side are bunched up pretty snug," Benteen mused.

"Can't you borrow some to place where they're needed?" his wounded first sergeant wanted to know.

Benteen nodded absently and patted the thickset McCurry reassuringly.

"I'll be back," he promised.

Benteen found the equivalent of a half a company hiding among the packs.

"Grab a box and a fistful of shells," he told them. "Report to Lieutenant Gibson. He'll put you to good use."

They were slow about responding.

He coaxed them with a genial smile. "Grab a box of bacon or hardtack and get on up there."

"We'll get killed," an anonymous soldier complained.

"Men," Benteen drawled, "this is a groundhog case; it's live or die with us. We must fight it out with them."

The motley crew began to move in the direction indicated. Two of them nearly tripped over Lieutenant Gibson in his hidey-hole.

"If he's in your way," Benteen suggested loudly, "boot him in the butt or walk right over him!"

The whole line within earshot was amused and even Gibson laughed good-naturedly as he pointed out positions to three C Company men led by Sergeant Knipe. The others were Private McGuire, who had helped recapture the stampeded mule the previous day, and his friend Peter Thompson, who had dropped out of the Custer column. Thompson had received an ugly flesh wound on his right biceps and was on his way to the hospital via the packs when Benteen found him. He went straight to the position indicated for him, his wound still undressed.

The Indians began snaking their way up the slopes, moving to within a stone's throw of H Company. In fact, many of them were throwing stones—and sticks and arrows and anything else that was handy.

The heavy fire from all points kept up and, within an hour, Benteen, sucking furiously on an unlit pipe, was towering over a very prone Major Reno.

"The Indians are doing their best to cut through my lines," he reported matter-of-factly. "It will be impossible for me to hold my position much longer."

Reno rolled over and popped his head up to stare at the very erect senior captain.

"What can I do?" Reno asked with a trace of exasperation.

"Some of these people are pretty well situated," Benteen told him evenly. "I think we should move a company out of the line and redistribute them where they're needed most."

"Go ahead, then," Reno told him impatiently.

"All right," Benteen called back over his shoulder as he strode away, "I will take French."

The bullets whizzed around the white-haired, pipe-chewing captain as he headed purposefully toward M Company. He didn't flinch or break stride. The troops watched his progress with open-mouthed amazement.

French agreed to move at once, but it was nearly a half hour before any of M Company moved. Benteen stopped near the packs to talk to Lieutenant Varnum.

"It's that son of a bitch Ryan," he complained. "I had him court-martialed for stringing a private up by the thumbs and busted him to the ranks. GAC thought better, however, and gave him back his stripes. Now, Ryan won't move his ass—he thinks he's getting back at me, I guess."

"Bust him again," Varnum snapped.

Benteen shook his head, smiling.

"No time for personal quarrels," he said. "We need Ryan and he *is* a good soldier. He'll come along when he's damn good and ready. He probably wants French to get the word from Reno."

"Where is the major?" Varnum wondered.

Benteen stared at his pipe with a tight smile. "He's in the same hole he was in when I saw him last."

"You shouldn't expose yourself like you do, Colonel."

Benteen raised his eyebrows as he replaced his pipe and began lighting it.

"Someone has to take charge," he said around puffs.

"You can't be much help to us dead," Varnum insisted.

"I can't be much help hiding in a hole with the rest of them," Benteen answered with a short laugh.

J. C. Wagner, the chief packer, was hit in the head by a spent bullet. He flopped around grotesquely, but before the others could reach him, he sat up, holding his head.

Private Herod Liddiard, a small loquacious Cockney, had been left with the packs for E Company. He had joined the motley crew Benteen had pressed into service on the hill. He lay prone, firing steadily and talking nonstop to himself.

Liddiard's chatter was a source of amusement to the men around him, and when he suddenly stopped talking, they crawled over to investigate. A single shot had drilled him through the forehead. The curious crawled away in silence.

Corporal George Lell from H Company was shot in the chest. As he was carried to the hospital and deposited on the blankets there, he forced himself up on his elbows, biting his lip in pain.

"Lift me up," he called. "I want to see the boys again before I go."

He was dutifully propped up after a nod of acquiescence from Dr. Porter and died a few minutes later, watching the "boys" fight off the steadily advancing Indians.

One Indian got so close to the lines that he was able to touch two bewildered troopers from H Company with a coup stick. A third soldier, Private Edward Pigford, shot him in the chest. The other two, galvanized, began to fire rapidly at the dead Indian's would-be rescuers.

Private Jasper Marshall of L Company had boots that didn't fit. After being sent to the H Company position by Captain Benteen, he lay prone, taking off his boots and setting them in front of him. He cringed involuntarily as another flight of arrows landed around his position with thuds. When he looked up, his ill-fitting boots were skewered to the ground.

"Hey, look!" he called in wonder to the man nearest him.

A dour corporal from H Company glanced over briefly.

"How did you get them off?" he asked, and returned to his own business.

Marshall regarded him with a puzzled frown. He scooted up

into a sitting position and almost fell over in shock. Another arrow was embedded in his left foot—right through the stocking.

Jasper Marshall began to laugh hysterically.

The flight of arrows that pinned Marshall's boots to the ground and wounded his ankle had taken a terrific toll of H Company. The arrows seemed to come from the ravine just west of the position, a spot that had hitherto been quiet.

The greatest damage was to nerves. First one and then several of the men began to run to the safety of the packs. Within minutes, half of Lieutenant Gibson's force had joined them as panic spread like a communicable disease.

Benteen's deep voice sounded like a trumpet above the din of consternation and reproach.

"Where are you running to, men?" he demanded.

He was answered with a sullen silence.

"C'mon back," he drawled, "and we will drive them back."

The dispirited men hesitated as if torn between terror and the call of duty.

"You might as well be killed out there as in here!" Benteen told them with a grin.

He led them back up the hill and stood behind them, watching, as First Sergeant Ryan belatedly led M Company reinforcements into the line. He walked up and down the line in full view of the Indian archers to the west. Arrows missed him and dirt clods and sticks landed on either side of him. He stooped and picked up a rock that had been hurled at him, regarding it in one hand and his pipe in the other. His genial grin vanished.

When he finally found his voice, it was loud and clear and carried over the field like a bullhorn.

"Now, men," he thundered, "I am getting damned mad! When I give the word—I want you to stand up and chase down the slope in full cry and skip them out!"

He paced a little, looking right and left and dropping the rock.

"Sound off like a thousand heathen Chinee. By God, we'll show these redskins a fight!"

He paused and drew in his breath like a bellows being inflated. The Indians were not idle. Arrows and bullets whipped past the white-haired old man who stood erect, watching.

He pumped his arm.

"Now's the time!" he yelled. "Hip! Hip! Here we go!"

In a mass, the men of H Company, their Falstaffian rein-forcements from the packs, the detachment from Captain French's M Company stood up and began running down the slope to the west, firing and screaming like banshees, albeit dry-throated banshees.

The yelling was a little weak and the shooting was wild and ineffective, but the Indians were "skipped out" by the sheer mass and shock of the charge. They tumbled like acrobats to find posi-tions of safety from the ragged, howling lines of Benteen's. Many ran pell-mell for the safety of the river.

Benteen trotted forward in the center behind the line of ad-vancing "Chinee."

"Hip! Hip!" he shouted, and troops answered, "Hurrah!"

Some were laughing hysterically. The advancing line was comi-cally ragged and the flight of the Indians looked somewhat hu-morous.

"Hip, hip, hurrah?" a young private from M Company called to the man on his left incredulously.

"The old man was in the Civil War," the other replied briefly by way of explanation.

Benteen whistled shrilly and, at his signal, flat-nosed John Mar-tin put his trumpet to his lips and sounded the urgent notes of the Recall.

The troops hurried back to their positions, not waiting around to see what the Indians thought of the maneuver. Benteen made his way back to a central position and stood watching them jog back up the hill and into the breastworks of boxes and packs they had left just minutes before.

He was smiling again.

Gerard and Jackson heard the racket from their position near the site of the first ford. They had tramped all night and ended up going in the opposite direction from the way they had taken initially. Daylight had found them in the trees facing Reno's first ford and they had decided to hole up there until dark.

They watched in alarm as a group of Indians trotted up on po-nies just behind them. The Indians seemed to be in conference.

One of them was set apart from the others, his horse and himself painted with red lightning flashes and hailstones. He was extremely light-complexioned and had a scar on his face. A single eagle feather was stuck in the back of his long black hair, which was braided Sioux-style with brown, fur-wrapped braids. He seemed covered with dust.

Gerard was distracted from studying the solitary Indian when Jackson touched his arm. The grizzled plainsman turned and saw a half dozen horsemen fording the river where Jackson's shaking finger was pointing. They reached the near side and galloped up to the solitary Indian, shouting in Lakota. The single Indian looked impassive, then grunted a few words inaudible to Gerard and his half-breed comrade and rode off in the direction of the Indian village without a backward glance.

Gerard watched as the riders returned to the river and crossed. The rest of the Indians studied the bluffs opposite for a time and then followed the trail of the solitary Indian back to the village. When they were a safe distance away, Gerard turned to Jackson.

"I think it was him," he whispered.

"Who?"

"Crazy Horse."

The fire slackened from the west and Benteen stared down the ravine he had charged with narrow-eyed thoughtfulness.

"Round up four or five of our best shots," he told Gibson peremptorily as he replaced his bow pipe in his mouth and turned toward the center of the perimeter.

Gibson looked puzzled, but ordered Sergeant George H. Geiger to report to him at once. Benteen disappeared in the direction of Moylan's A Company.

Geiger was a short, burly, fair-haired man of thirty-three. His light eyes seemed to have no life in them as he crouched in front of Gibson.

"The old man wants some sharpshooters out front," Gibson told Geiger. "Pick three good men and stand by."

"What are we going to be shooting at, sir?"

"I don't know," Gibson replied. "When the old man gets back, he'll explain what he wants done."

Geiger nodded and hurried down the line, picking up two other

H Company men, hustling them toward the crude trench that had been dug the night before. The two men were Otto Voit, a short, swarthy German immigrant who worked as a saddler, and Henry W. B. Mecklin, a beefy youngster who was a blacksmith.

Private Charles Windolph, the dark, neat little German tailor with a wounded buttock, had already established himself in the "trench." He didn't ask questions as the others joined him, but shook hands with Voit without breaking his rhythm of firing and reloading.

Benteen explained his "idee" to Moylan. The sandy-mustachioed A Company commander with the gun-barrel eyes nodded.

"We'll send them down twelve at a time," Benteen repeated. "All volunteers, from wherever we can get them. You round up the volunteers on this side. I'll get some from the other side. And give them all the kettles you can spare."

Moylan nodded as Benteen strolled casually away. Sergeant Culbertson, A Company's acting first sergeant, appeared beside Moylan.

"A water party," Moylan explained. "We need volunteers."

"Who's leading it, sir?"

"Colonel Benteen suggested it. It's up to him."

Culbertson nodded.

"Sergeant Roy!" he called. "We need volunteers again."

"It occurred to me after we had charged down the slope," Benteen explained to Major Reno and Dr. Porter at the hospital. "Mr. Lo deserted one of the ravines almost completely as far as I can see. I think they'll be slow about filling it up again. They don't care for our dismounted cavalry charges." He laughed shortly, obviously relishing the memory.

"I don't know," Reno said uncertainly.

"Some of the wounded are going to die without water," Dr. Porter said.

"It's no bigger a gamble than our little charge," Benteen told them as he sauntered away.

Reno nodded after the stocky figure of Benteen as he addressed Dr. Porter.

"You can thank God he's on the hill with us," he said quietly.

In groups of two, the volunteers reported to Captain Benteen on the reverse slope of H Company's position. They carried kettles—six altogether—and each man had two gray felt-covered quart canteens.

"The volunteers are ready when you are, sir," Lieutenant Gibson reported, gesturing toward the mounds of earth dug up at the far left of the line.

"I want them to walk down the slope to the head of the ravine and fire into anything between them and the river," Benteen told him.

Gibson gulped.

"Do they know this?" Benteen prodded.

"They will, sir."

Gibson instructed a young private nearby to crawl to the end of the line and relay the plan to the four sharpshooters. As the private dutifully made his way down the line, Benteen took his pipe out of his mouth and stared hard at the recumbent Gibson. He didn't say anything for a long time. Gibson was unable to hold the stare. When Benteen finally spoke, his voice was flat and tight.

"Watch the line like a mother hen, Gib. Keep some of the guns firing east too. Our volunteers are going to slip down that ravine to the west and bring back some water for our wounded."

The volunteers inched forward, drawing a fusillade of fire.

"Dammit, I told you to keep down," Benteen told them crossly. "Now, keep down!"

"Captain, sorr," Michael Madden from K Company shouted back over the din of the fire, "ye tell us to keep down. It's yourself should keep down. They'll get ye."

Benteen puffed on his pipe until the nervous laughter and Indian fire both died somewhat, then raised his voice so that it could be heard up and down the line.

"No," he called, "Mother sewed some good medicine in my tunic before we came out." He modeled his rumpled blue shirt dramatically, waving his pipe for emphasis. "They dare not hit me."

The men laughed and cheered.

There were an even dozen volunteers waiting to dash down the ravine to the west on Benteen's command and fill their canteens and kettles in the Little Big Horn River below. Moylan's A Company was the best represented and it was Sergeant Roy, the picket-line commander of the previous night for that company, that Benteen turned to when it came time to give instructions.

"Use your best judgment when you get to the bottom," the pipe-puffing senior captain told the dark little Frenchman. "Maybe go two at a time, maybe three at a time, I don't know. Are you ready?"

Roy nodded and looked back over his water party. Three privates from his own Company A accompanied him. John Gilbert, the hazel-eyed young Irishman, was first. Neil Bancroft, the fair-haired New Yorker, and David Harris, the florid-faced Indiana farm boy, followed. All three had been up all night with Sergeant Roy on the picket line. Peter Thompson, the C Company dropout, was with them. The dark-haired, ruddy-faced Scotsman had been slightly wounded in the right biceps and the wound had not been treated, but he concealed it by rolling down his sleeve and jogged down the ravine with the others.

B Company was represented by two men, Private Boren and Private Coleman. Tiny G Company, with none to spare, sent a young man named Theo Goldin. Goldin was eighteen, a runaway from Wisconsin, who doubled as regimental clerk. A large-eyed, thin-nosed youngster, he hurried down the ravine in the company of large, black-haired Michael Madden from K Company.

"What's Madden doing volunteering?" Lieutenant Gibson asked Benteen. "I thought all he was good for was carousing and occupying the guardhouse."

Benteen shrugged, not taking the pipe from his lips. "He is a rather intemperate fellow," he remarked, puffing.

Gibson rolled his eyes at the comment from the rather intemperate senior captain.

"I'm very much surprised," he said neutrally.

Otto Voit, the small, dark German saddler from H Company, handed his carbine to Windolph as the sharpshooters neared the ravine. Behind him, one of the volunteers was making his way back to the lines. Voit joined the water party in the ravine without any comment—or consent being given. No one protested.

The last two men down the slope were M Company privates named James Tanner and James Wilber. Tanner was dark-eyed and deeply tanned; Wilber, blue-eyed and red-faced.

In the ravine—which was devoid of Indians at least for the time being—the party was safe from hostile fire. The three remaining marksmen at the top of the hill overlooking the ravine fired nonstop at targets of opportunity that presented themselves at the river and in the wooded area across and beyond. The twelve men were able to slip down into the ravine without being hit from behind due to the covering fire from the rest of Gibson's men aiming at the east. The going was rough and their being overladen with receptacles didn't speed up their progress any.

Still, the first real danger they encountered was at the river. They dashed to the water one at a time. The first two men filled up two-gallon camp kettles without incident and, retreating twenty yards to the relative safety of the ravine, allowed the others to drink their fill and transfer water from their canteens to the kettles.

Beefy Mike Madden was the third to go and, on the return from the river, fell heavily. He had been shot in the leg.

"Leave me, boys," he protested when they tried to lift him and carry him back up the ravine.

"I don't know why a big lummox like you came down in the first place," a voice from the rear offered uncharitably.

"Aye," Madden replied with a weak grin, his heavy dark face sweating profusely. "It's not for meself, that's for sure. But the poor boys up there are cryin' for the wather, and what could I do?"

Sergeant Roy studied the west bank and the brush to the north of their hiding place.

"We'll wait a bit," he told the tense volunteers.

"We had to tie down Crowley," young Gilbert remarked to no one in particular. "He'd gone crazy from the thirst."

"Our boys are eatin' grass up there," one of the men from B Company contributed.

They waited and watched, discussing the situation among themselves with a quiet air of desperation.

At the head of the ravine, the rest of the command was not idle. Sergeant Fehler, an elderly German immigrant from M Company, reported to Benteen with three additional sharpshooters.

"Sergeant Ryan said you might need us, sir."

Benteen, staring anxiously at the ravine, pointed his pipestem toward the head of the ravine where Geiger and the two remaining H Company marksmen were standing and firing.

"If my people can keep the reds off your back, think you can throw lead at the timber in the bottom?"

Sergeant Fehler inflated his not so small chest and nodded. The four reinforcements raced out into the open and took up standing and kneeling positions at the top of the ravine with Sergeant Geiger's party. There they had an unrestricted view of the river below and the timber on the west side where the harassing fire had pinned down Sergeant Roy's water party.

The renewed heavy burst of firing from the head of the ravine galvanized the trapped water party. Private Wilber of M Company and the doughty Sergeant Roy ran to the river and threw themselves prone, lapping up water and filling their canteens as they lay there. They rolled away and ducked back up the ravine. Wilber was hit in the left ankle, but managed to hobble to safety without spilling a drop of water.

The long wait had taken its toll of the nerves of the others, but Roy's leadership broke the impasse. They began to dash to the river once again at regular intervals. Altogether, they filled six kettles holding two gallons each and numerous one-quart canteens.

They started back up the ravine, the kettle bearers leading and the trailing four men carrying the badly wounded Madden. Wilber hobbled along behind, alone. They dropped Madden twice and his howls could be heard above the crack of carbines clear across the other side of the perimeter.

"That's Madden," K Company's sole remaining trumpeter, George Penwell, remarked to Godfrey. Godfrey nodded. Down along the line of Madden's company, others began to laugh and then to cheer.

The jubilation was picked up by parched throats all over the perimeter as the twelve men and the two bands of sharpshooters covering scampered back to relative safety. The water party made it to the hospital area bearing the precious water and a howling Madden.

Dr. Porter took charge of the water and began doling it out to the wounded. Benteen placed Lieutenant Varnum in charge of what was left.

"Guard it with your life," he told the pinch-faced scout commander–adjutant.

The intensity of fire from the north and east increased following the return of the water party. All along the line, dead horses and mules were piled up as ghastly breastworks. The wounded ones were cut loose and driven out of the compound. The bodies of the dead animals bloated in the scorching sun, and with each round of firing, the hiss of escaping gas could be heard as bullets plowed into the ripe bodies. The stench was horrid. Benteen made his way to Reno's side.

"You must do something about things on your side pretty quick," he said without preamble. "This won't do. You must drive them back."

Reno muttered and Benteen strode away.

As he passed K Company, Lieutenant Hare called out.

"You're drawing the fire, Colonel Benteen!"

Benteen stopped to consider the matter and grinned broadly.

"Well," he drawled loudly, "they fire about so often anyway."

The troops within earshot laughed and began to cheer.

Even normally expressionless Ed Godfrey grinned.

"We have charged the Indians from our side and driven them out," Benteen called to Reno a second time. "They are coming to our left and you ought to drive them out."

Reno sat up and looked around.

Benteen was standing on the slope of the finger-shaped hill above Moylan's line and exposed to the Indians' heaviest fire.

"Can you see the Indians from there?" Reno called back.

Benteen looked innocently at the impacting rounds close to where he was standing.

"Yes!" he yelled with a grin.

"If you can see, then give the command," Reno told him.

All along Moylan's line, the listening troopers sat up in anticipation. Lieutenant Varnum abandoned the nearly depleted water reserves and moved in among them, signaling for them to crouch preparatory to charging.

Benteen paced, throwing his bull-like voice up and down the lines.

"Those bastards up there are shooting right into you!" he informed the waiting men.

"We want to skip them out!" he went on, watching the ridge where the Indians were firing from. "Is it a go?"

"It's a go!" The soldiers' response was cracked and dry. They shifted and began to shuffle forward at a crouch.

"Give them hell!" Benteen roared.

He waved his arm in the signal. Moylan's A Company and Wallace's G Company rose as one and rushed forward, yelling like men possessed. Weir's D Company and Godfrey's K Company followed suit.

Reno was in the middle and, as he topped the rise, a bullet zipped past him on the ground. He ducked involuntarily and then straightened with a laugh.

"Damned if I want to be killed by an Indian now," he told Godfrey with a grin. "I've gone through too many fights for that!"

The charge didn't carry more than a hundred yards, and to all appearances the cavalrymen didn't inflict a single casualty, but the Indians massing in front of Moylan fled in three directions and the sharpshooters that had galled H Company from the rear since the evening of the previous day abandoned their positions.

Trumpeter Penwell of K Company blew the Recall at Major Reno's command. All the attacking soldiers made it back without incident except one. Frenetic Lieutenant Charles Varnum had to be helped back. His buckskinned legs were bleeding below the knees.

"I'm okay!" he assured Benteen, who hurried over toward him. "Just a little Indian buckshot in the legs is all. No serious damage. I'm okay."

"You'd better let Doc Porter be the judge of that, young man," Benteen said gruffly. He clapped the tall, thin Varnum affectionately on the shoulder and turned his attention to the west.

The Indian sniper fire had diminished and the arrows had stopped altogether.

From the western side, one sniper in particular was making life miserable for M Company.

"He's got a rifle," First Sergeant John Ryan reported to Captain French. "A muzzle loader is my guess from the time he takes between shots. He's up in that tree yonder and he's got the range now."

"What tree?" Tucker French demanded, squinting.

Ryan pointed to one almost at the base of the bluffs opposite, a good six hundred yards away. French whistled.

"He got Varner in the ear and Rutten in the right shoulder," Ryan went on. "Earlier, he got Sergeant Carey in the hip—a bad wound. He seems to be hitting every third man. I thought you'd like to know."

"Why?"

"You're next in rotation," Ryan informed his superior with a grim smile.

French grinned.

"Well, Sergeant Ryan, we'll just have to do something about that!"

The two men stood up and moved forward—French with his .50-caliber Springfield and Ryan with a Sharps buffalo rifle. They both fired at the tree.

Six hundred yards or more away, the sniper was hit in the hip and fell from the tree, breaking his neck. French and Ryan saw him fall. They shook hands.

"You got him, Captain," Ryan congratulated French.

"No," French replied seriously, "I was high. It must have been you."

From behind them came an exasperated, anonymous voice.

"For Chrissake, will you two get down?"

A bullet whipped through French's hat, the impact taking it off. The slab-faced commander of M Company leaned over and retrieved it, poking his finger through the entry hole.

"Boys, that was a pretty close shave," he called out. "I guess it's about time I should make a move!"

He and Ryan returned to cheers and laughter.

With monotonous regularity, the wounded men were carried from points on the line to the crude little hospital that Dr. Porter had established in the center of a ring of mules—some of them dead—that Lieutenant Mathey had made the previous night. Private Peter Thompson finally decided to have his arm attended to and received a bawling out from harried Dr. Porter that seemed more painful to the ears of the listeners than the bullet could possibly have been to Thompson's arm. The tough little Scots dropout from Custer's column grinned and nodded agreement with the frustrated medical man.

White Swan, the big-bellied Crow who had argued with Custer the previous morning at the Crow's Nest, was hauled back from the firing line by a couple of Captain McDougall's men. The Indian scout had been shot in the hand by a cavalryman in the valley—an ugly, crippling wound—and had been hit in the legs five or six times by Indian snipers on the hill. He refused medical attention and persisted in dragging himself back into the line, grabbing tufts of grass with his only good hand and pushing his Winchester rifle ahead of him with his chin. After a dozen frustrated attempts, he continued to try to crawl forward. The concerned men from B Company finally gave up and let him go forward.

Benteen heard the cries for water from the wounded on one of his many trips through the hospital area and walked straight to Captain McDougall and French, who were huddled together.

It had sprinkled again briefly after Reno's charge about noon, but within an hour the dusty, smoky battlefield was scorching hot from the sun that was hidden to view by the man-made cloud of gunpowder.

"We need more water," Benteen told the two company commanders.

"Another water party?" French asked.

Benteen nodded.

"Another charge." McDougall's voice was heavy with resignation and irony. But there was something else in his voice in that moment as well—a touch of awe.

Benteen nodded, grinning widely from habit.

McDougall smiled back tiredly.

"Well, Fred," he told the ragged-looking white-haired man in front of him, "there's no need to stand on a hill and tell us when it's safe to go. Just give us time to get ready and point us in the right direction. We'll take things from there. You've done enough already."

"This time," Benteen told the others, "I'll have the volunteers standing by. We'll all go together."

"Let us know when you're ready," McDougall said again.

Benteen refused permission for any of the first water party to volunteer for a second try. The new volunteers assembled, carrying the battered kettles and festooned once again with quart canteens. B Company supplied the noncom to lead the party—Sergeant Rufus D. Hutchinson, a tall, young Ohio farmer with fair hair and a thick Custer mustache. He was accompanied by a raw young Irishman named Thomas Callan and a quiet, deadly Englishman named Jim Pym.

D Company provided the bulk of the volunteers. Lieutenant Edgerly had little trouble finding any. A lanky Kentuckian named Bill Harris stepped forward and took up a kettle without the nod of approval from First Sergeant Martin.

"You're due for a discharge, Private Harris," Edgerly said quietly.

"I want to go, Lieutenant," the man replied earnestly.

"You don't have to," Edgerly persisted.

"I want to," Harris answered a second time, impatiently. He was joined by Private George D. Scott.

"Not both of you," Sergeant Martin protested.

"Lieutenant," Scott appealed to Edgerly, "Bill and I are from the same home town. We enlisted together. We're going home together. We do everything together."

"There's no point in dying together," Edgerly said kindly.

"If he goes, I go," Scott said stubbornly.

Edgerly raised his eyebrows in appeal to Sergeant Martin. The old noncom shrugged, hiding a grin.

"Carry on," Edgerly told the two veterans crisply.

Three New Yorkers joined the Kentuckians with the same argument. Edgerly nodded stiffly, his clear eyes twinkling. The three were Abraham Brant, Frank Tolan, and Charles Welch.

The last man from D Company to join was a tall, husky German blacksmith named Frederick Deitline.

"I can't refuse you," Edgerly told the assembled volunteers. "God bless you, men."

Lanky Lieutenant Nick Wallace had gathered around him some of the survivors of the disaster in the valley, so that G Company was no longer represented by a mere three men. In addition to the strays he had picked up the previous evening, Wallace had been assigned many of the men from the packtrain details of the five companies Custer had led downstream.

Private Thomas Stevenson, a red-headed, ruddy-faced Irishman was allowed by Wallace to join the second water party. He was accompanied by a very young Iowa farm boy with blond hair and a red face named Charles Campbell. The two men from G Company reported to Captain Benteen, who was superivsing preparations for the charge behind McDougall's B Company. The Indian fire was heavy only on that side of the perimeter.

Private James Weeks, a tall young Canadian recruit from M Company, was the last volunteer to join the water party, which had assembled in the relative safety of the area to the rear of B and H Companies to be briefed by Lieutenant Frank Gibson.

"When I give the signal," Gib told the twelve men, "you run forward, slither through the high grass, tumble down the ravine ass over camp kettle, fill everything that will hold it with water, and come back as fast as you can run. Any questions?"

There were no questions.

"The first group went two at a time to the river," Lieutenant Gibson offered. "I'd recommend that you do the same. Now, we'll give you as much support as we can, but if the going gets rough, remember: you're volunteers. I can't compel you to go. That is, I won't compel you—"

He broke off self-consciously as he studied the faces of the twelve men, who didn't blink at the prospects. Gibson cleared his throat.

"Wait for the word," he said, "and—good luck."

The fire had diminished on the other side of the perimeter and two of the G Company men that had been in the group led out of the timber by George Herendeen crawled forward to get better positions to fire at the disappearing targets. Andrew J. Moore stood up.

"Get down," his buddy, Hugh McGonigle, remonstrated.

"I can see better this way," Moore answered.

A split instant later, an Indian rifle shot struck him in the chest. He crumpled and was dead before McGonigle could drag himself the five yards to his side.

Sergeant Daniel Knipe had remained in the H Company line since joining them that morning. As he looked up from where he crouched, he saw the burly shoulders and long white hair of Captain Fred Benteen. Benteen's eyes were red and his lips were cracked and bleeding, but he stood erect as the bullets from the Indian snipers snapped around his open blue shirt, which had worked out of his trousers and hung disreputably over his hips. He was sucking his right thumb, which had been struck only minutes before by a spent bullet. His empty pipe was clutched in his left hand.

"Do you desire to draw the Indian fire?" Knipe asked Benteen.

"If they are going to get you," Benteen replied, spitting his wounded thumb out with a weary sigh, "they will get you somewhere else if not here."

Benteen remained rooted for a long time in the spot and then, just as it seemed to Knipe that the fire around him was slackening, he turned and walked away in the direction of French's M Company.

Captain Benteen had his now bandaged right hand stuck nonchalantly in the waistband of his sagging trousers and he nodded to the cluster of trumpeters he had assembled. The trumpets began to blow the clarion call of the Charge and, simultaneously, B and M Companies spilled out from behind their crude barricades and swarmed down the slopes to the west and south, yelling hoarsely and firing wildly.

As before, the Indians retreated precipitately. Benteen, watching, waved his left arm in a signal to Lieutenant Gibson. The water party started out just as the two companies were trotting back in response to the Recall that Benteen now had the trumpeters play.

Private Campbell, the little Iowa farm boy from G Company, with hit in the right shoulder almost immediately. He fell heavily, striking his head. Four watching H Company men dashed out to drag the wounded youngster back.

"Go on, boys," he protested weakly. "I can make it back some way."

But they ignored him and one of the rescuers, a twenty-four-year-old recruit from Ohio named Jacob Adams, joined the water party without waiting for permission. He paused only to take the canteens from the wounded man. Campbell was carried back to the hospital.

The Indians were a little quicker about getting back into position after this third charge. Dark-eyed James Tanner of M Company almost made it back to safety, but not quite. He slipped and fell, a bullet through the chest.

"Bring him in!" a voice called.

"Bring him in!" thirty voices took up the cry.

Sergeant John M. Ryan and three other men grabbed a large saddle blanket between them and dashed out into the exposed grass and rolled the unfortunate Tanner into the blanket. They staggered back up the slope with Indian bullets tearing the air around them.

When they unrolled their burden at the stark hospital, one of them whispered to the dying man, "Poor Tanner, they got you now."

"No," Tanner replied weakly, "but they will have in a few minutes."

The water party was accompanied by the same four sharpshooters from H Company. They dashed down the slope into the head of the ravine. Mecklin, Voit, Windolph, and Sergeant Geiger kept up a steady stream of fire atop the ravine.

The bullets whistled past the heads of Lieutenant DeRudio and Private O'Neill crouched among the tree roots at the southern end of the little island. Their pursuers had given up long before, but the two men could hear Indians talking between their own position and the hill where the fire was coming from.

"Damn!" O'Neill whispered as another round whipped past him. "This has got to be the longest day of my life."

DeRudio nodded ambiguously.

"Wait unteel night," he advised.

The water party raced forward four at a time. The first four would lie down and take in as much water as they dared, while the canteens they carried were allowed to dangle in the water. They filled the kettles with one casual swipe of the wrist, dragging them through the unresisting water. They rolled away from the river's edge and bounded back up the narrow ravine.

The water was churned up considerably with Indian bullets and shots from the four H Company sharpshooters that fell short. One of the kettles was filled as much with lead as water and it dripped water as it was carried back up the ravine.

The last group waited barely five seconds and they too were gone. The last man up the slope for the miraculously unhit water party was the tall Canadian, Jim Weeks, from M Company.

"Let me have a little sip of that water," Captain Myles Moylan told Weeks as the young water carrier arrived at the hospital area to turn over his portion to Lieutenant Varnum.

"You go to hell!" Weeks told Moylan fiercely. "This water is for the wounded."

Moylan flushed angrily, but said nothing.

Shortly afterward, the Indians left.

The fire from the west side began to lighten up after the return of the second water party. The fire from the east side had stopped altogether. The men of the 7th Cavalry ate from the rations the mules had carried and watched, not daring to stick their heads up too high.

Sporadic firing continued from the west side without doing damage to either side for almost two hours. It was nearly seven in the evening before the besieged soldiers saw the reason.

A long column of Indians, bearing their earthly possessions on their backs or on the backs of their ponies travois-style, filled the valley floor as the entire camp came into view headed south by west in the direction of the Big Horn Mountains.

The soldiers stood up to watch the procession.

"There must twenty thousand horses in that herd," Lieutenant Hare remarked for the second time in as many days. This time, Lieutenant Godfrey looked at his young second lieutenant with renewed respect.

Major Reno hurried over to where Captain McDougall was standing and pointing at the huge column of Indians moving away from the battlefield.

"Where are they going?" Reno asked, shading his eyes with his palm.

"Upstream," McDougall answered placidly.

"They're going away," a young trooper sobbed in relief.

Others began to cheer halfheartedly.

"It's probably only a ruse to get us on the move so they can clean us out," an M Company private behind a bacon box told Sergeant Ryan.

Ryan shook his head, but didn't speak.

Across the perimeter, Lieutenant Edgerly was coming to the same conclusion.

"I think they are short of ammunition and are moving the village to safety before making a last desperate attempt to overwhelm us," he told a white-faced Captain Weir.

Weir regarded the big young second lieutenant out of the corner of his eye.

"You're wrong," he said flatly.

"We won! We won!" a B Company sergeant kept repeating over and over again.

Lieutenant Gibson and Captain McDougall joined an exhausted-looking Captain Benteen. The senior captain's tunic was in disarray and outside his waistband. With the cool breeze of the early evening flapping it gently, he began to tuck it in, gingerly favoring his wounded hand.

"Well, Fred," McDougall asked quietly, "did we do it or not?"

Benteen stared bleakly at the column of Indians that had become mostly dots and dust on the horizon.

"We survived," he grunted.

Captain French bustled up, his coal-black eyes glowing.

"We did it! We held our own!" he announced. "Though I must say their poor marksmanship was our salvation."

"From where I fought," Lieutenant Gibson remarked crankily, "their marksmanship wasn't all that bad. We lost too many men to them."

Captain McDougall was quick to agree.

"And they just kept coming," he added with awe. "I think they used every blade of grass down there and some of them twice. And they just kept coming."

French appealed to Benteen, who had hunched down into a crouch wearily and was dry-washing his face with his hands.

"What about it, Fred?" French demanded brusquely. "Good shots or bad shots?"

Benteen's normally deep voice was strangely soft as he answered without taking his eyes off the horizon.

"Good shots," he said, "good riders . . . and the best damn fighters the sun ever shone on."

Night—
Monday, June 26, 1876

The night was darker than the one before. The Indians had shown no signs of returning and the survivors would have remained where they were had it not been for the stench of the dead horses and mules—and men.

Major Reno looked annoyedly at the hospital a few yards away where a young private from H Company named George cried out in agony. His cry was not exactly choked off, but it came to a sudden, throbbing stop.

"I think it is safe to send additional water parties down to the river, don't you?" Reno asked of a thoroughly exhausted Benteen. Benteen smothered his tenth yawn in as many minutes and nodded, his large, pale blue eyes watering with the effort.

"Let's move the whole thing toward the river," he suggested almost lifelessly. "We can cover the approach to the water and still command the high ground."

"I don't think the men can be pushed for another minute's labor," Reno objected.

Benteen's massive head raised from his chest and he straightened his back as he sat cross-legged in front of Reno. His large blue eyes were no longer hooded with weariness.

"With their own hair at stake," he said, "they might have wings."

"Well," said Reno placatingly, "you do what you think best."

Benteen posted McDougall's B Company on the south side of the water carriers' ravine and Captain Moylan's A Company on the north side. He instructed them to encircle their position with a trench.

They worked in relays—some sleeping, some standing guard, some digging the sandy Montana soil. Moylan and McDougall had them relieved frequently, so that while the greatest percentage of their time was devoted to catching long-neglected sleep, security was not relaxed and work went on using every piece of entrenching equipment they were able to scrounge.

Volunteers made repeated trips to the river to fill canteens and kettles and just to immerse their own parched, dusty faces in the cooling water. After a time, Benteen allowed Mathey to supervise the watering of a few of the more restless horses. The watering scene was pathetic. The animals plunged their heads into the water up past their eyes and heaved and snorted raucously. They tried to roll in the water, but Mathey's handlers wouldn't permit it.

The firing had long ended, the Indians appeared to be completely gone and it had been dark almost an hour. Gerard and Jackson left their cover and swam across the river. On the far shore, Jackson started to move off. Gerard caught him by the arm.

"This way," he whispered loudly, pointing up the water carriers' ravine. "There was an Army patrol or something down here this afternoon, remember?"

The two men trudged up the hill and were challenged by a picket from A Company.

"Gerard!" Gerard shouted back. "And Billy Jackson, scout!"

"Advance, Gerard and Billy-Jackson-Scout and be recognized," the cavalryman called out mechanically.

Lieutenant Varnum was among the first to greet them.

"Have you seen Lieutenant DeRudio?" he asked.

"We split up last night a little north of here—near the river," Gerard replied. "He had a G Company man named Tom O'Neill with him. We haven't seen them since last night."

A husky corporal came up carrying blankets.

"Thank you," said Gerard. "By the way, I stepped on a dead Indian on the way up. He's layin' just over there." He gestured.

Six men trotted off in the indicated direction.

"He's already been scalped!" one of them cried out in disappointment.

Sergeant Benjamin C. Criswell, the dark little West Virginian who had refused to leave the lines to be treated for a neck wound the first day and who had spent most of the second day hauling ammunition to the lines fully exposing himself to the Indian fire, volunteered to lead the burial party.

The burial party was for little Lieutenant Benny Hodgson and was Captain Mac's idea. The roly-poly commander of Company B took charge of the party himself at the last moment. It consisted of McDougall, Sergeant Criswell, and three privates.

They reached the body, finding it where Varnum had left it on the evening of the twenty-fifth. McDougall supervised the loading of his second lieutenant's body into two Army blankets sewn together and helped lower the bundle into a shallow grave at the base of the bluff. They marked it crudely with sticks and returned slowly to the top of the hill to report the accomplishment to Major Reno.

DeRudio and O'Neill hugged the west shore of the Little Big Horn until they came to the spot where Jackson and Gerard had crossed an hour earlier and where Major Reno and three companies of cavalry and thirty scouts had crossed two interminable afternoons before.

Once on the east bank, they began walking slowly toward the lone tepee. From off to their left, a mule brayed loudly.

"Hear that?" O'Neill demanded, grabbing the wet tunic of the thoroughly bedraggled Italian dandy.

"I can't hear," DeRudio answered.

"It was a mule. I'm sure of it. The rest of the command must be over that direction somewheres."

Dubiously, DeRudio accompanied the young man who had been his companion for one day and a half and two long nights.

A few minutes later, they heard the voice of Trumpeter McVeigh lifted in anger.

DeRudio lost all doubt. He raced forward, outdistancing O'Neill.

"Mac!" he shouted. "Hey, McVeigh! It's me—Lieutenant DeRudio! And—" He turned to O'Neill puffing behind him. "What was your name?" he whispered.

"ONeill!" O'Neill shouted for himself, not breaking stride even though it was rough terrain and pitch-black. "Private O'Neill—G Company! And Lieutenant DeRudio!"

A zombie-like picket let them pass, but it was a delirious Lieutenant Varnum who greeted them when they came in.

Tuesday, June 27, 1876

The sun had been up almost three hours before Major Reno gave permission for the rest of the horses and mules to be watered. It was even more pathetic than the previous night. There were more animals and it was broad daylight. The beasts slid down the ravine in places on their haunches in their frantic hurry to get to the water. They plunged their muzzles into the river up to the eyes and drank and frolicked noisily. It was a veritable mob scene with the soldiers attempting to control their animals' movements and at the same time allow them to water ahead of the others. The soldiers lost control. Many gave up in disgust and took to the water themselves. One of Godfrey's K Company men went a little downstream to avoid the crowd. He knelt and was about to plunge his face in the river when his eye caught something brown in the water. He stood up in alarm and watched in horror as the bloated body of a horse long dead bobbed to the edge of the river where he was standing.

Some of the water parties and horses were still at the river when the pickets spotted it. A long column of riders was moving through the abandoned Indian village following the course of the river upstream.

Long-legged Lieutenant Nick Wallace came running up to Major Reno. Reno was watching the advance of the new group of riders near the village when Wallace pointed him in the direction of the high ground they had briefly occupied on the evening of the twenty-fifth. A much smaller group of horsemen was headed directly for the 7th Cavalry's position.

"Could this be General Custer?" Reno wondered out loud.

"Captain Weir saw them through Flanagan's glasses and he says they're not naked, but wearing blue," Wallace informed him.

"Some of the Indians are wearing blue," Fred Gerard warned.

"Lieutenant Godfrey and Lieutenant Hare are mounted and want to ride out to investigate," Wallace told Reno. "I'd like to go with them."

"Tell them to go with drawn pistols," Reno advised the lanky acting commander of G Company. "If there're hostiles, get back here at once."

Wallace bobbed his head and loped back across the perimeter to where Godfrey and Hare were waiting, mounted.

Godfrey recognized the lead rider as Lieutenant James H. Bradley of Gibbon's 7th Infantry. He looked on impassively as Wallace and Hare shook hands enthusiastically with a strangely pale Bradley.

"Where is Custer?" Godfrey demanded abruptly.

Bradley couldn't meet his eagle's gaze.

"I don't know," he said quietly, "but I suppose he was killed. . . . We counted a hundred and ninety-seven bodies. . . . I don't suppose any escaped."

The three officers from the 7th were speechless.

A few minutes later, General Alfred H. Terry rode up the water carriers' ravine accompanied by his staff and escort. His basset hound face was solemn and his eyes watered at the sight of the pitiful scarecrow figures who emerged from their trenches and barricades to cheer. He stopped in front of Major Reno and Captain Benteen.

Reno was unable to give voice to his thoughts and Terry was equally speechless. Benteen was the first to speak.

"Where is Custer?" he asked brusquely.

Terry's reply was low-pitched and oddly humble.

"To the best of my knowledge and belief, he lies on this ridge about four miles below here . . . with all his command killed."

There was a shocked silence as the cheering and hubbub died abruptly. In the eerie silence, Benteen's hoarse voice could be heard by all.

"I can hardly believe it," Benteen rasped. "I think he is somewhere down the Big Horn grazing his horses. At the Battle of the

Washita, he went off and left a part of his command and I think
he would do it again."

Terry looked stricken.

"I think you are mistaken," he said very quietly, his eyes mist-
ing again, "and you will take your command and go down where
the dead are lying and investigate for yourself."

Even in his shock, there was no mistaking the authority of the
general's command.

DeRudio asked to come along as Benteen supervised preparations for the move to the ridge where Terry's scouts had reported
the dead bodies.

"If you can find a horse," Benteen murmured distractedly.

"Corporal Pahl is wounded," Lieutenant Frank Gibson informed the little Italian. "You can ride his horse."

The column under Benteen was led by Lieutenant Godfrey and
Captain Weir, and they stopped at the peaks they had abandoned
so precipitately two days before. Godfrey studied the field that
had been covered with dust and smoke when they had looked at
it on the twenty-fifth. His field glasses seemed glued to his eyes.

Even without glasses, the rest of them could see little white
specks dotting the green and brown hillside, much like boulders.

"What are those?" was the question that penetrated Godfrey's
ears above the murmurs and exclamations.

He dropped his glasses as if they had burned his eyes.

"The dead!" he said loudly in the unnatural silence that followed.

Behind him, Captain Weir's voice broke.

"Oh, how white they look!" he said. "How white!"

The column walked on, down the coulee and over the high
ridge between it and the battlefield.

As the survivors of the 7th Cavalry fanned out across the battlefield searching for survivors and dead bodies, Lieutenant Varnum posted the remaining scouts and a small patrol of cavalrymen on a high hill to the east with instructions to watch for
Indians.

"My punishment for tampering with Reno's precious message,"

he remarked to Billy Jackson with a scornful laugh. He kept his pinched face glued to the blue lines working over the hill among the white and brown clumps that were all he could see of the dead.

Big Lieutenant Edgerly and the rest of D Company worked the south end of the long ridge. There they found the bodies of Calhoun's L Company in almost perfect skirmish-line order. The dead bodies were bloated badly and most were unrecognizable, but the cries of the men under his supervision told Edgerly that individuals were being identified.

A pale sergeant directed his attention to two bodies near the center of the knoll.

"Lieutenant Calhoun," Edgerly pronounced after studying the fillings in the teeth of a naked body with blond hair.

The second body pointed out to him was filled with arrows—including one in an eye. Edgerly looked away.

"Lieutenant Crittenden," he muttered.

Captain Weir, working a little ahead of Edgerly and on the east slope of the steep ridge, found I Company. He sent a galloper after Benteen.

When the senior captain appeared in response to the summons, Weir pointed at a cluster of white and partially blackened bodies, mutilated almost beyond recognition.

"Myles Keough," he reported succinctly. "You can tell by the medal around his neck. One of my boys recognized the trumpeter lying across him. Sergeant Varden's here too. And Bustard. Looks like they were ambushed in a group."

Benteen was testy as he took the "Pro Petri Sede" medal Weir had secured from Keough's mutilated body.

"I see no evidence of first-class fighting anywhere," he growled. "If anything, they appear to have been handled worse than Reno's battalion in the bottom—if that is possible."

Weir nodded dully.

"This is what we saw two days ago under that cloud of dust. We should have come on. Ignored Reno, I mean." Weir looked uncertainly at Benteen. The white-haired man was nodding wearily.

"Reno should have stayed in the bottom. Once he came out, we had no choice but to go to his assistance. If he had attacked the village as he was ordered, I doubt if this would have happened. It looks like the reds just swarmed over them in column."

He looked aside to Lieutenant Hare, who was taking in the opinions of the two veteran captains with open-mouthed astonishment.

Captain Thomas McDougall looked into the deep gully that was filled with dead bodies. He looked away quickly and questioned his first sergeant with a fractionally uplifted eyebrow.

"It's the Gray Horse," First Sergeant James Hill, a middle-aged Scotsman, murmured. "E Company. Hohmeyer is there and Moonie, but I can't see Mr. Sturgis or Lieutenant Smith."

"Smith is up on the hill," McDougall answered, nodding sympathetically as First Sergeant Hill shook his head in perplexity. "It makes no sense," he agreed.

Hare and Benteen rode over to the hill Godfrey and Wallace were working.

"They didn't find Jimmy Porter," Hare ventured. "I wonder if he got away."

Benteen shook his head emphatically.

"Two hundred men well fought should have made a better showing," he said, as if in answer to an unspoken question.

"There appears to have been a stand here," Godfrey told Benteen as he arrived with Hare. Wallace joined them in surveying the top of the small knoll with a ring of dead horses.

"The rest of them are scattered between here, the river, and where Captain McDougall's people are working now," he reported. "This looks like it was Tom Custer's command."

"We found the general," Godfrey told Benteen quietly as if he had not heard Wallace.

Benteen stared at the naked body of Custer, which was lying as if sleeping across the chest of another body.

"His wounds were cleaned," Benteen observed, pointing to the bullet holes in Custer's side and temple that showed no trace of powder or blood.

Wallace examined another body in the center of the ring of dead horses. "It's Tom Custer," he declared.

Benteen looked at the indicated body with revulsion. It had been disemboweled and lay face up in the hot sun, totally naked. The back of the head had been smashed in savagely and the facial features were unrecognizable. The back and head had been filled with arrows, including one that two enlisted men were unable to remove from the top of the head.

"How can you tell?"

"The tattoo on the wrist. It's Tom Custer all right."

Benteen looked away.

"They cut Cookey's beard off," Godfrey said.

"He was right here at the end," Benteen agreed in a wondering voice. He handed Godfrey the medal Weir had recovered from Keough's body. Godfrey passed it back.

"Keough?"

Benteen nodded grimly.

"Did any of them get away?" Wallace wondered out loud.

Godfrey surveyed the carnage dispassionately.

"I don't think so," he said very, very quietly.

Wednesday, June 28, 1876

The burials were indecent by any standards. The torn and hacked and bloated bodies were covered over hastily with a pitiful layer of dirt and rocks—and sometimes tree branches nearer the river. More time and effort was spent marking the graves than making them. The bodies of those officers identified were tagged by writing their names on pieces of paper and sticking them inside empty cartridge cases which were inserted in the ground next to sticks that marked the head of the graves.

Godfrey covered over Boston Custer while a corporal beside him covered up young Autie Reed's remains. Atop the small knoll, the only proper grave of the battlefield was being dug, for Brevet Major General George Armstrong Custer. DeRudio's young companion in the bottom, Private Thomas F. O'Neill, and another G Company man named John E. Hammon dug Custer's grave with the only two spades on the hill. Wallace prepared the marker consisting of a slip of paper inside a carbine cartridge case screwed into the sandy soil next to a small piece from an Indian lodgepole.

Captains Fred Benteen and Thomas Weir watched the burial from horseback a few yards away. O'Neill hesitated as he was about to secure the blanket around Custer's naked body preparatory to lowering it into the shallow hole he and Hammon had dug. He glanced at the watching officers as if for a signal.

Lieutenant Nick Wallace screwed up his kind but homely face against the sun and cleared his throat. Weir was weeping soundlessly.

For a long time no one spoke or moved. Then Benteen shifted.

When he spoke, his voice was thick with emotion. More in sorrow than in anger, he pronounced the benediction O'Neill seemed to be waiting for.

"There he is, goddam him, he will never fight again."

BOOKS that proved of use to the author
and, therefore,
could prove of interest to the reader . . .

Ambrose, Stephen. *Crazy Horse and Custer*. Doubleday, 1975.

Bates, Charles Francis. *Custer's Indian Battles*. Privately printed, 1936.

Brady, Cyrus T. *Indian Fights and Fighters*. University of Nebraska Press, 1971.

Brininstool, Earl. *Troopers with Custer*. Stackpole, 1952.

Brown, Dee. *Showdown at the Little Bighorn*. Putnam's, 1964.

Carroll, John M. *The Benteen-Goldin Letters on Custer and His Last Battle*. Liveright, 1974.

Chandler, Melbourne C. *Of Garryowen and Glory: The History of the Seventh United States Cavalry*. Privately printed, 1960.

Coffeen, Herbert. *The Custer Battle Book*. Carleton, 1964.

Custer, Elizabeth B. *Boots and Saddles; or, Life in Dakota with General Custer*. Harper & Bros., 1885.

Dustin, Fred. *The Custer Tragedy*. Edward Bros., 1939.

Ege, Robert J. *Curse Not His Curls*. Old Army Press, 1973.

Fougera, Katherine Gibson. *With Custer's Cavalry*. Caxton Printers, 1940.

Frost, Lawrence. *The Custer Album: A Pictorial Biography of Custer*. Superior, 1964.

Graham, W. A. *The Custer Myth: A Source Book of Custeriana*. Stackpole, 1953.

——. *Abstract of the Reno Court of Inquiry*. Stackpole, 1954.

Gray, John S. *Centennial Campaign: The Sioux War of 1876*. Old Army Press, 1976.

K

Greene, Jerome A. *Evidence and the Custer Enigma.* Outbooks, 1973.

Hammer, Ken. *Men with Custer: Biographies of the 7th Cavalry.* Old Army Press, 1972.

———. *Custer in '76: Walter Camp's Notes on the Custer Fight.* Brigham Young University Press, 1976.

Hutchins, James S. *Boots and Saddles at the Little Bighorn.* Old Army Press, 1976.

Kuhlman, Charles. *Custer and the Gall Saga.* Old Army Press, 1972.

———. *Legend into History.* Stackpole, 1951.

Luce, Edward S. *Keough, Comanche & Custer.* Swift, 1939.

Merington, Marguerite. *The Custer Story.* Devin-Adair, 1950.

Miller, David Humphries. *Custer's Fall.* Duell, Sloan & Pearce, 1957.

Monaghan, Jay. *Custer: The Life of George Armstrong Custer.* Little, Brown, 1959.

Reedstrom, E. Lisle. *Bugles, Banners and Warbonnets.* Caxton Printers, 1977.

Roe, Charles Francis. *Custer's Last Battle.* Robert Bruce, 1927.

Stewart, Edgar I. *Custer's Luck.* University of Oklahoma Press, 1955.

Terrell, John Upton, and Walton, George. *Faint the Trumpet Sounds.* McKay, 1966.

Utley, Robert M. *Life in Custer's Cavalry.* Yale University Press, 1977.

———. *Custer Battlefield.* National Park Service, 1967.

van de Water, Frederick. *Glory Hunter.* Bobbs-Merrill, 1934.

Vaughn, J. W. *Indian Fights: New Facts on Seven Encounters.* University of Oklahoma Press, 1966.

Fw
M   Mills, Charles K.
        A mighty afternoon

DISCARD